Mary Hartwell Catherwood

Mackinac and lake Stories

Mary Hartwell Catherwood

Mackinac and lake Stories

ISBN/EAN: 9783743348738

Manufactured in Europe, USA, Canada, Australia, Japa

Cover: Foto ©Andreas Hilbeck / pixelio.de

Manufactured and distributed by brebook publishing software (www.brebook.com)

Mary Hartwell Catherwood

Mackinac and lake Stories

[Page 222

" THAT WAS THE MOMENT OF LIFE "

MACKINAC AND LAKE STORIES

By

MARY HARTWELL CATHERWOOD

WITH ILLUSTRATIONS

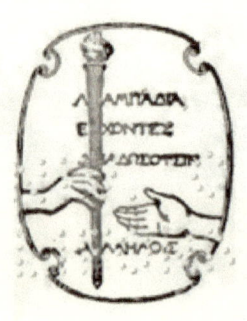

HARPER & BROTHERS PUBLISHERS
NEW YORK AND LONDON

TO

My Dear Daughter

HAZEL

THE COMPANION OF ALL MY JOURNEYS

CONTENTS

ILLUSTRATIONS

MARIANSON

WHEN the British landed on the west side of Mackinac Island at three o'clock in the morning of July 17, 1812, Canadians were ordered to transport the cannon. They had only a pair of six-pounders, but these had to be dragged across the long alluvial stretch to heights which would command the fortress, and sand, rock, bushes, trees, and fallen logs made it a dreadful portage. Voyageurs, however, were men to accomplish what regulars and Indians shirked.

All but one of the hundred and sixty Canadians hauled with a good will on the cannon ropes. The dawn was glimmering. Paradise hid in the untamed island, breathing dew and spice. The spell worked instantly upon that one young voyageur whose mind was set against the secret attack. All night his rage had been swelling. He despised the British regulars—forty-two lords of them only being in this expedition—as they in turn despised his class. They were his conquerors. He had no desire to be used as means of pushing their conquest further. These islanders he knew to be of his own race, perhaps crossed with Chippewa blood.

Seven hundred Indians, painted and horned for war, skulked along as allies in the dim morning twilight. He thought of sleeping children roused by tomahawk and scalping-knife in case the surprised fort did not immediately surrender. Even then, how were a few hundred white men to restrain nearly a thousand savages?

The young Canadian, as a rush was made with the ropes, stumbled over a log and dropped behind a bush. His nearest companions scarcely noticed the desertion in their strain, but the officer instantly detailed an Indian.

"One of you Sioux bring that fellow back or bring his scalp."

A Sioux stretched forward and leaped eagerly into the woods. All the boy's years of wilderness training were concentrated on an escape. The English officer meant to make him a lesson to the other voyageurs. And he smiled as he thought of the race he could give the Sioux. All his arms except his knife were left behind the bush; for fleetness was to count in this venture. The game of life or death was a pretty one, to be enjoyed as he shot from tree to tree, or like a noiseless-hoofed deer made a long stretch of covert. He was alive through every blood drop. The dewy glory of dawn had never seemed so great. Cool as the Sioux whom he dodged, his woodsman's eye gathered all aspects of the strange forest. A detached rock, tall as a tree, raised its colossal altar, surprising the eye like a single remaining temple pillar.

Old logs, scaled as in a coat of mail, testified to the humidity of this lush place. The boy trod on sweet white violets smelling of incense.

The wooded deeps unfolded in thinning dusk and revealed a line of high verdant cliffs walling his course. He dashed through hollows where millions of ferns bathed him to the knees. As daylight grew — though it never was quite daylight there—so did his danger. He expected to hear the humming of an arrow, and perhaps to feel a shock and sting and cleaving of the bolt, and turned in recklessly to climb for the uplands, where after miles of jutting spurs the ridge stooped and pushed out in front of itself a round-topped rock. As the Canadian passed this rock a yellow flare like candle-light came through a crack at its base.

He dropped on all-fours. The Indian was not in sight. He squirmed within a low battlement of serrated stone guarding the crack, and let himself down into what appeared to be the mouth of a cave. The opening was so low as to be invisible just outside the serrated breastwork. He found himself in a room of rock, irregularly hollow above, with a candle burning on the stone floor. As he sat upright and stretched forth a hand to pinch off the flame, the image of a sleeping woman was printed on his eyeballs so that he saw every careless ring of fair hair around her head and every curve of her body for hours afterwards in the dusk.

His first thought was to place himself where his

person would intercept any attack at the mouth of the cave. Knife in hand, he waited for a horned, glittering-eyed face to stoop or an arrow or hatchet to glance under that low rim, the horizon of his darkness. His chagrin at having taken to a trap and drawn danger on a woman was poignant; the candle had caught him like a moth, and a Sioux would keenly follow. Still, no lightest step betrayed the Sioux's knowledge of his whereabouts. A long time passed before he relaxed to an easy posture and turned to the interior of the cave.

The drip of a veiled water-vein at the rear made him conscious of thirst, but the sleeping woman was in the way of his creeping to take a drink. Wrapped in a fur robe, she lay breathing like an infant, white-skinned, full-throated, and vigorous, a woman older than himself. The consequences of her waking did not threaten him as perilous. Without reasoning, he was convinced that a woman who lay down to sleep beside a burning candle in this wild place would make no outcry when she awoke and found the light had drawn instead of kept away possible cave-inhabitants. Day grew beyond the low sill and thinned obscurity around him, showing the swerve of the roof to a sloping shelf. Perspiration cooled upon him and he shivered. A fire and a breakfast would have been good things, which he had often enjoyed in danger. Rowing all night, and landing cannon at the end of it, and running a league or more for life, exhausted a man.

4

"SHE LAY BREATHING LIKE AN INFANT"

The woman stirred, and the young voyageur thought of dropping his knife back into its sheath. At the slight click she sat up, drawing in her breath.

He whispered: "Do not be afraid. I have not come in here to hurt you."

She was staring at him, probably taking him for some monster of the dark.

"Have you anything here to eat?"

The woman resumed her suspended breath, and answered in the same guarded way, and in French like his: "Yes. I come to this part of the island so often that I have put bread and meat and candles in the cave. How did you find it? No one but myself knew about it."

"I saw the candle-light."

"The candle was to keep off evil spirits. It has been blown out. Where did you come from?"

"From St. Joseph Island last night with the English. They have taken the island by surprise."

She unexpectedly laughed in a repressed gurgle, as a faun or other woods creature might have laughed at the predicaments of men.

"I am thinking of the stupid American soldiers —to lie asleep and let the British creep in upon them. But have you seen my cow? I searched everywhere, until the moon went down and I was tired to death, for my cow."

"No, I saw no cow. I had the Sioux to watch."

"What Sioux?"

"The Indian our commandant sent after me. Speak low. He may be listening outside."

5

They themselves listened.

"If Indians have come on the island they will kill all the cattle."

"There are the women and children and men—even poor voyageurs—for them to kill first."

She gasped, "Is it war?"

"Yes, it is war."

"I never have seen war. Why did you come here?"

"I did not want to, mademoiselle, and I deserted. That is why the Indian was sent after me."

"Do not call me mademoiselle. I am Marianson Bruelle, the widow of André Chenier. Our houses will be burned, and our gardens trampled, and our boats stolen."

"Not if the fort surrenders."

Again they harkened to the outside world in suspense. The deserter had expected to hear cannon before sunlight so slowly crept under the cave's lip. It was as if they sat within a colossal skull, broad between the ears but narrowing towards the top, with light coming through the parted mouth. Accustomed to the soft twilight, the two could see each other, and the woman covertly put her dress in order while she talked.

More than fearlessness, even a kind of maternal passion, moved her. She searched in the back of the cave and handed her strange guest food, and gathered him a birch cup of water from the dripping rock. The touch of his fingers sent a new vital thrill through her. Two may talk together under the same roof for many years, yet never really meet; and two others at first speech are old friends. She did not know this young voyageur, yet she began to claim him.

He was so tired that the tan of his cheek turned leaden in the cave gloom. She rose from her bear-skin and spread it for him, when he finished eating.

"You cannot go out now," he whispered, when he saw her intention. "The Sioux is somewhere in the woods watching for me. The Indians came on this island for scalps. You will not be safe, even in the fort, until the fight is over, or until night comes again."

Marianson, standing convinced by what he said, was unable to take her eyes off him. Mass seemed always irksome to her in spite of the frequent changes of posture and her conviction that it was good for her soul. She was at her happiest plunging through woods or panting up cliffs which squaws dared not scale. Yet enforced hiding with a stranger all day in the cave was assented to by this active sylvan creature. She had not a word to say against it, and the danger of going out was her last thought. The cavern's mouth was a very awkward opening to crawl through, especially if an Indian should catch one in the act. There was nothing to do but to sit down and wait.

A sigh of pleasure, as at inhaling the spirit of a flower, escaped her lips. This lad, whose presence she knew she would feel without seeing if he came into church behind her, innocent of the spell he

was casting, still sat guarding the entrance, though
the droop of utter weariness relaxed every posture.
Marianson bade him lie down on the fur robe, and
imperiously arranged her lap to hold his head.

"I am maman to you. I say to you sleep, and
you shall sleep."

The appealing and thankful eyes of the boy
were closed almost as soon as he crept upon the
robe and his head sunk in its comfortable pillow.
Marianson braced her back against the wall and
dropped her hands at her sides. Occasionally she
glanced at the low rim of light. No Indian could
enter without lying flat. She had little dread of
the Sioux.

Every globule which fell in darkness from the
rock recorded, like the sand grain of an hour-glass,
some change in Marianson.

"I not care for anybody, me," had been her
boast when she tantalized soldiers on the village
street. Her gurgle of laughter, and the hair blowing on her temples from under the blanket she
drew around her face, worked havoc in Mackinac.
To her men were merely useful objects, like cows,
or houses, or gardens, or boats. She hugged the
social liberty of a woman who had safely passed
through matrimony and widowhood. Married to
old André Chenier by her parents, that he might
guard her after their death, she loathed the thought
of another wearisome tie, and called it veneration
of his departed spirit. He left her a house, a cow,
and a boat. Accustomed to work for him, she

found it much easier to work for herself when he was gone, and resented having young men hang around desiring to settle in her house. She laughed at every proposal a father or mother made her. No family on the island could get her, and all united in pointing her out as a bad pattern for young women.

A bloom like the rose flushing of early maidenhood came over Marianson with her freedom. Isolated and daring and passionless, she had no conception of the scandal she caused in the minds of those who carried the burdens of the community, but lived like a bird of the air. Wives who bore children and kept the pot boiling found it hard to see her tiptoeing over cares which swallowed them. She did not realize that maids desired to marry and she took their lovers from them.

But knowledge grew in her as she sat holding the stranger's head in her lap, though it was not a day on which to trouble one's self with knowledge. There was only the forest's voice outside, that ceaseless majestic hymn of the trees, accompanied by the shore ripple, which was such a little way off. Languors like the sweet languors of spring came over her. She was happier than she had ever been before in her life.

"It is delicious," she thought. "I have been in the cave many times, but it will never be like this again."

And it was a strange joy to find the touch of a human being something to delight in. There was sweet wickedness in it; penance might have to follow. What would the curé say if he saw her? To amuse one's self with soldiers and islanders was one thing; to sit tranced all day in a cave with a stranger must be another.

There was a rough innocence in his relaxed body —beautiful as the virgin softness of a girl. Under the spell of his unconscious domination, she did not care about his past. Her own past was nothing. She had arrived in the present. Time stood still. His face was turned towards her, and she studied all its curves, yet knew if he had other features he would still be the one person in the world who could so draw her. What was the power? Had women elsewhere felt it? At that thought she had a pang of anguish and rage altogether new to her. Marianson was tender even in her amusements; her benevolence extended to dumb cattle; but in the hidden darkness of her consciousness she found herself choosing the Sioux for him, rather than a woman.

Once he half raised his head, but again let it sink to its rest. Marianson grew faint; and as the light waned at the cave mouth she remembered she had not eaten anything that day. The fast made her seem fit to say prayers, and she said all she knew over his head, like a mother brooding.

He startled her by sitting up, without warning, fully roused and alert.

"What time is it?" inquired the boy.

" Look at the door. The sun has long been behind the trees."

" Have I slept all day ?"

" Perhaps."

" And have you heard no sound of battle ?"

"It has been still as the village street during
mass."

" What, then, have they done, those English ?
They must have taken the fort without firing a
gun. And the Sioux—you have not seen him ?"

" Nothing has passed the cave door, not even a
chipmunk."

He stretched his arms upward into the hollow,
standing tall and well made, his buckskin shirt
turned back from his neck.

" I am again hungry."

" I also," said Marianson. " I have not eaten
anything to-day."

Her companion dropped on his knees before her
and took out of her hands the food she had ready.
His face expressed shame and compunction as he
fed her himself, offering bites to her mouth with
gentle persistence. She laughed the laugh peculiar
to herself, and pushed his hand back to his own lips.
So they ate together, and afterwards drank from
the same cup. Marianson showed him where the
drops came down, and he gathered them, smiling at
her from the depths of the cave. They heard the
evening cawing of crows, and the waters rushing
with a wilder wash on the beach.

" I will bring more bread and meat when I come

back," promised Marianson—"unless the English have burned the house."

"No. When it is dark I will leave the cave myself," said the voyageur. "Is there any boat near by that I can take to escape in from the island?"

"There is my boat. But it is at the post."

"How far are we from the post?"

"It is not so far if one might cross the island; but to go by the west shore, which would be safest, perhaps, in time of war, that is the greater part of the island's girth."

They drew near together as they murmured, and at intervals he held the cup to her lips, making up for his forgetfulness when benumbed with sleep.

"One has but to follow the shore, however," said the boy. "And where can I find the boat?"

"You cannot find it at all."

"But," he added, with sudden recollection, "I could never return it again."

Marianson saw on the cave's rough wall a vision of her boat carrying him away. Her own little craft, the sail of which she knew how to trim—her bird, her flier, her food-winner—was to become her robber.

"When the war is over," she ventured, "then you might come back."

He began to explain difficulties like an honest lad, and she stopped him. "I do not want to know anything. I want you to take my boat."

He put the cup down and seized her hands and kissed them. She crouched against the cave's side, her eyes closed. If he was only grateful to her for bread and shelter and means of escape, it was little enough she received, but his warm touch and his lips on her palms—for he kissed her palms—made her none the less dizzy.

"Listen to me," said Marianson. "If I give you my boat, you must do exactly as I bid you."

"I promise."

"You must stay here until I bring it to you. I am going at once."

"But you cannot go alone in the dark. You are a woman—you will be afraid."

"Never in my life have I been afraid."

"But there are Indians on the war-path now."

"They will be in camp or drunk at the post. Your Sioux has left this part of the island. He may come back by morning, but he would not camp away from so much plunder. Sioux cannot be unlike our Chippewas. Do you think," demanded Marianson, "that you will be quite, quite safe in the cave?"

Her companion laughed.

"If I find the cave unsafe I can leave it; but you in the dark alone—you must let me go with you."

"No; the risk is too great. It is better for me to go alone. I know every rock, every bend of the shore. The pull back around the island will be hardest, if there is not enough wind."

"I go with you," decided the boy.

"But you gave me your promise to do exactly as I bade you. I am older than you," said Marianson.

"I know what is best, and that is that you remain here until I come. Swear to me that you will."

He was silent, beseeching her with his eyes to relent. Then, owning her right to dominate, he pledged her by the name of his saint to do as she required.

Their forced companionship, begun at daylight, was ending as darkness crept through the cavern's mouth. They waited, and those last moments of silence, while they leaned to look closely at each other with the night growing between them, were a benediction on the day.

Marianson stooped to creep through the cavern's mouth, but once more she turned and looked at him, and it was she herself who stretched appealing arms. The boy's shyness and the woman's aversion to men vanished as in fire. They stood together in the hollow of the cave in one long embrace. He sought her mouth and kissed her, and, suffocating with joy, she escaped through the low door.

Indifferent to the Indian who might be dogging her, she drew her strip of home-spun around her face and ran, moccasined and deft-footed, over the stones, warm, palpitating, and laughing, full of physical hardihood. In the woods, on her left, she knew there were rocks splashed with stain black as ink and crusted with old lichens. On her right white-caps were running before the west wind and diving like ducks on the strait. She crossed the threads of a brook ravelling themselves from density. For the forest was a mask. But Marianson knew well the tricks of that brook—its pellucid shining on pebbles, its cascades, its hidings underground of all but a voice and a crystal pool. Wet to her knees, she had more than once followed it to its source amid such greenery of moss and logs as seemed a conflagration of verdure.

The many points and bays of the island sped behind her, and cliffs crowded her to the water's edge or left her a dim moving object on a lonesome beach. Sometimes she heard sounds in the woods and listened; on the other hand, she had the companionship of stars and moving water. On that glorified journey Marianson's natural fearlessness carried her past the Devil's Kitchen and quite near the post before she began to consider how it was best to approach a place which might be in the hands of an enemy. Her boat was tied at the dock. She had the half-ruined distillery yet to pass. It had stood under the cliff her lifetime. As she drew nearer, cracks of light and a hum like the droning of a beehive magically turned the old distillery into a caravansary of spirits.

Nothing in her long tramp had startled her like this. It was a relief to hear the click of metal and a strange-spoken word, and to find herself face to face with an English soldier. He made no parley, but marched her before him; and the grateful noise of squalling babies and maternal protests and Maman Pelott's night lullaby also met her as they proceeded towards the distillery.

The long dark shed had a chimney-stack and its

many-coiled still in one end. Beside that great bot-
tle-shaped thing, at the base of the chimney, was
an open fireplace piled with flaming sticks, and
this had made the luminous crevices. All Mackinac
village was gathered within the walls, and Marianson beheld a camp supping, putting children to bed
on blankets in corners, sitting and shaking fingers
at one another in wrathful council, or running about
in search of lost articles. The curé was there, keeping a restraint on his people. Clothes hung on
spikes like rows of suicides in the weird light.
Even fiddlers and jollity were not lacking. A
heavier race would have come to blows in that
strait enclosure, but these French and half-breeds,
in danger of scalping if the Indians proved turbu-
lent, dried their eyes after losses, and shook their
legs ready for a dance at the scraping of a violin.

Little Ignace Pelott was directly pulling at Marianson's petticoat to get attention.

"De Ingins kill our 'effer," he lamented, in the
mongrel speech of the quarter-breed. "Dey didn't
need him; dey have plenty to eat. But dey kill
our 'effer and laugh."

"My cow, is it also killed, Ignace?"

Marianson's neighbors closed around her, unsur-
prised at her late arrival, filled only with the general calamity. Old men's pipe smoke mingled with
odors of food; and when the English soldier had
satisfied himself that she belonged to this caldron
of humanity, he lifted the corners of his nose and
returned to open air and guard duty.

The fort had been surrendered without a shot, to save the lives of the villagers, and they were all hurried to the distillery and put under guard. They would be obliged to take the oath of allegiance to England, or leave the island. Michael Dousman, yet held in the enemy's camp, was fiercely accused of bringing the English upon them. No, Marianson could not go to the village, or even to the dock.

Everybody offered her food. A boat she did not ask for. The high cobwebby openings of the distillery looked on a blank night sky. Marianson felt her happiness jarred as the wonderful day came to such limits. The English had the island. It might be searched for that young deserter waiting for her help, and if she failed to get a boat, what must be his fate?

She had entered the west door of the distillery. She found opportunity to slip out on the east side, for it was necessary to reach the dock and get a boat. She might risk being scalped, but a boat at any cost she would have, and one was sent her—as to the fearless and determined all their desires are sent. She heard the thump of oars in rowlocks, bringing the relief guard, and with a swish, out of the void of the lake a keel ran upon pebbles.

So easy had been the conquest of the island, the British regular found his amusement in his duty, and a boat was taken from the dock to save half a mile of easy marching. It stood empty and waiting during a lax minute, while the responsibility of guarding was shifted; but perhaps being carelessly beached, though there was no tide on the strait, it drifted away.

Marianson, who had helped it drift, lay flat on the bottom and heard the rueful oaths of her enemies, forced to march back to the post. There was no sail. She steered by a trailing oar until lighted distillery and black cliff receded and it was safe for her to fix her sculls and row with all her might.

She was so tired her heart physically ached when she slipped through dawn to a landing opposite the cave. There would be no more yesterdays, and there would be no time for farewells. The wash which drove her roughly to mooring drove with her the fact that she did not know even the name of the man she was about to give up.

Marianson turned and looked at the water he must venture upon, without a sail to help him. It was not all uncovered from the night, but a long purple current ran out, as if God had made a sudden amethyst bridge across the blue strait.

Reluctant as she was to call him from the cave, she dared not delay. The breath of the virgin woods was overpoweringly sweet. Her hair clung to her forehead in moist rings, and her cheeks were pallid and wet with mist which rose and rose on all sides like clouds in a holy picture.

He was asleep.

She crouched down on cold hands and saw that. He had waited in the cave as he promised, and had fallen asleep. His back was towards her. Instead of lying at ease, his body was flexed. Her enlarging pupils caught a stain of red on the bear-skin, then the scarlet tonsure on his crown. He was asleep, but the Sioux had been there.

The low song of wind along that wooded ridge, and the roar of dashing lake water, repeated their monotone hour after hour. It proved as fair a day as the island had ever seen, and when it was nearly spent, Marianson Bruelle still sat on the cave floor holding the dead boy in her arms. Heart-uprooting was a numbness, like rapture. At least he could not leave her. She had his kiss, his love. She had his body, to hide in a grave as secret as a flower's. The curé could some time bless it, but the English who had slain him should never know it. As she held him to her breast, so the sweet processes of the woods should hold him, and make him part of the island.

THE BLACK FEATHER

OVER a hundred voyageurs were sorting furs in the American Fur Company's yard, under the supervision of the clerks. And though it was hard labor, lasting from five in the morning until sunset, they thought lightly of it as fatigue duty after their eleven months of toil and privation in the wilderness. Fort Mackinac was glittering white on the heights above them, and half-way up a paved ascent leading to the sally-port sauntered 'Tite Laboise. All the voyageurs saw her; and strict as was the discipline of the yard, they directly expected trouble.

The packing, however, went on with vigor. Every beaver, marten, mink, musk-rat, raccoon, lynx, wild-cat, fox, wolverine, otter, badger, or other skin had to be beaten, graded, counted, tallied in the company's book, put into press, and marked for shipment to John Jacob Astor in New York. As there were twelve grades of sable, and eight even of deer, the grading, which fell to the clerks, was no light task. Heads of brigades that had brought these furs from the wilderness stood by to challenge any mistake in the count. It was the

20

height of the fur season, and Mackinac Island was the front of the world to the two or three thousand men gathered in for its brief summer.

Axe strokes reverberated from Bois Blanc, on the opposite side of the strait, and passed echoes from island to island to the shutting down of the horizon. Choppers detailed to cut wood were getting boat-loads ready for the leachers, who had hulled corn to prepare for winter rations. One pint of lyed corn with from two to four ounces of tallow was the daily allowance of a voyageur, and the endurance which this food gave him passes belief.

Étienne St. Martin grumbled at it when he came fresh from Canada and pork eating. "Mange'-du-lard," his companions called him, especially Charle' Charette, who was the giant and the wearer of the black feather in his brigade of a dozen boats. Huge and innocent primitive man was Charle' Charette. He could sleep under snow-drifts like a baby, carry double packs of furs, pull oars all day without tiring, and dance all night after hardships which caused some men to desire to lie down and die. The summer before, at nineteen years of age, this light-haired, light-hearted voyageur had been married to 'Tite Laboise. Their wedding festivities lasted the whole month of the Mackinac season. His was the Wabash and Illinois River outfit, almost the last to leave the island; for the Lake Superior, Upper and Lower Mississippi, Lake of the Woods, and other outfits were obliged to seek Indian hunting-grounds at the earliest breath of autumn.

21

When the Illinois brigade returned, his wife, who had stood weeping in the cheering crowd while his companions made islands ring with the boat-song at departure, refused to see him. He went to the house of her aunt Laboise, where she lived. Mademoiselle Laboise, her half-breed cousin, met him. This educated young lady, daughter of a French father and Chippewa mother, was dignified as a nun in her dress of blue broadcloth embroidered with porcupine quills. She was always called Mademoiselle Laboise, while the French girl was called merely 'Tite. Because 'Tite was married, no one considered her name changed to Madame Charette. To her husband himself she was 'Tite Laboise, the most aggravating, delicious, unaccountable creature in the Northwest.

"She says she will not see you, Charle'," said Mademoiselle Laboise, color like sunset vermilion showing in the delicate aboriginal face.

"What have I done?" gasped the voyageur.

Mademoiselle lifted French shoulders with her father's gesture. She did not know.

"Did I expect to be treated this way?" shouted the injured husband.

"Who can ever tell what 'Tite will do next?"

That was the truth. No one could tell. Yet her flightiest moods were her most alluring moods. If she had not been so pretty and so adroit at dodging whippings when a child, 'Tite Laboise might not have set Mackinac by the ears as often as she did. But her husband could not comfort himself with this thought as he turned to the shop of madame her aunt, who was also a trader.

It had surprised the Indian widow, who betrothed her own daughter to the commandant of the fort, that her husband's niece would have nobody but that big voyageur Charle' Charette. Though in those days of the young century a man might become anything; for the West was before him, an empire, and woodcraft was better than learning. Madame Laboise accepted her niece's husband with kindness. Her house was among the most hospitable in Mackinac, and she was chagrined at the reception the young man had met.

He sat down on her counter, whirling his cap and caressing the black feather in it. The gentle Chippewa woman could see that his childish pride in this trophy was almost as great as his trouble. What had 'Tite lacked? he wanted to know. Had he not good credit at the stores? Tonnerre!—if madame would pardon him—was not his entire year's wage at the girl's service? Had he spent money on himself, except for tobacco and necessary buckskins? Madame knew a voyageur was allowed to carry scarce twenty pounds of baggage in the boats.

Did 'Tite want a better man? Let madame look at the black feather in his cap. The crow did not fly that could furnish a quill he could not take from any man in his brigade. Charle' threw out the arch of his beautiful torso. And he loved her. Madame knew what tears he had shed, what serenades he had

23

played on his fiddle under 'Tite's window, and how he had outdanced her other partners. He dropped his head on his breast and picked at the crow's feather.

The widow Laboise pitied him. But who could account for 'Tite's whims? "When she heard the boats were in sight she was frantic with joy. I myself," asserted madame, "saw her clapping her hands when we could catch the song of the returning voyageurs. It was then 'Oh, my Charle'! my Charle'!' But scarce have the men leaped on the dock when off she goes and locks the door of her bedroom. It is 'Tite. I can say no more."

"What offended her?"

"I know of nothing. You have been as good a husband as a voyageur could be. And Mackinac is so dull in winter she can amuse herself but little. It was hard for her to wait your return. Now she will not look at you. It is very silly."

What would Madame Laboise advise him to do?

Madame would advise him to wait as if nothing had occurred. The curé would admonish 'Tite if she continued her sulking. In the mean time he must content himself with tenting or lodging among his fellow-voyageurs.

Of the two or three thousand voyageurs and clerks, one hundred lived in the agency house, five hundred were accommodated in barracks, but the majority found shelter in tents and in the houses of the villagers. Every night of the fur-trading month there was a ball in Mackinac, given either by the

householders or their guests; and it often happened
that a man spent in one month all he had earned
by his year of tremendous and far-reaching toil.
But he had society, and what was to him the cream
of existence, while it lasted. He fitted himself out
with new shirts and buckskins, sashes, caps, neips,
and moccasins, and when he was not on duty
showed himself like a hero, knife in sheath, a weath-
er-browned and sinewy figure. To dance, sing,
drink, and play the violin, and have the scant dozen
white women, the half-breeds, and squaws of Mackinac admire him, was a voyageur's heaven—its brief
duration being its charm. For he was a born
woodsman and loved his life.

Charle' Charette did not care where he lodged.
Neither had he any heart to dance, until he looked
through the door of the house where festivities began that season and saw 'Tite Laboise footing it
with Étienne St. Martin. Parbleu! With Étienne
St. Martin, the squab little lard-eater whose brother,
Alexis St. Martin, had been put into doctors' books
on account of having his stomach partly shot away,
and a valve forming over the rent so that his diges-
tion could be watched. It was disgusting. 'Tite
would not speak to her own husband, but she would
come out before all Mackinac and dance with any
other voyageurs who crowded about her. Charle'
sprang into the house himself, and without looking
at his wife, hilariously led other women to the best
places, and danced with every sinuous and graceful
curve of his body. 'Tite did not look at him. From

THE BLACK FEATHER

the corner of his eye he noted how perfect she was, the fiend! and how well she had dressed herself on his money. All the brigades knew his trouble by that time, and an easy breath was drawn by his entertainers when he left the house with knife still sheathed. In the wilderness the will of a brigade commander was law; but when the voyageur was out of the Fur Company's yard in Mackinac his own will was law.

One of the cautious clerks suggested that Charle' and Étienne be separated in their work, since it was likely the husband might quarrel with 'Tite Laboise's dancing partner.

"Turn 'em in together, man," chuckled the Scotch agent, Robert Stuart, who had charge of the outside work. "Let 'em fight. Man Gurdon, I havena had any sport with these wild lads since the boats came in."

But the combatants he hoped to see worked steadily until afternoon without coming to the grip. They had no brute Anglo-Saxon antagonism, and being occupied with different bales, did not face each other.

The triple row of Indian lodges basked on the incurved beach, where a thousand Indians had gathered to celebrate that vivid month. Night and day the thump of their drums and the monotonous chant of their dances could be heard above the rush and whisper of blue water breaking on pebbles.

Lake Michigan was a deep sapphire color, and

from where she stood below the sally-port 'Tite Laboise could see the mainland's rim of beach and slopes of forest near and distinct in transparent light. And she could hear the farthest shaking of echoes from island to island like a throb of some sublime wind instrument. The whitewashed block-house at the west angle of the fort shone a marble turret. There was a low meadow between the Fur Company's yard and pine heights. Though no salt tang came in the wind, it blew sweet, refreshing the men at their dog-day labor. And all the spell of that island, which since it rose from the water it has held, lay around them.

Étienne St. Martin picked up a beaver-skin, and in the sight of 'Tite Laboise her husband laid hold of it.

" Release that, Mange'-du-lard," he said.

" Eh bien !" responded Étienne, knowing that he was challenged and the eyes of the whole yard were on him. " This fine crow he claims all Mackinac because he carries a black feather in his cap. There are black feathers in other brigades."

" But you never wore one in any brigade."

They dropped the skin and faced each other, feeling the fastenings of their belts. Old Robert Stuart slipped up a window in the office and grinned slyly out at the men surging towards that side of the yard. He would not usually permit a breach of discipline. But the winter had been so long !

" Myself I have no need of black feathers."

27

Étienne gave an insolent cast of the eye to the height where 'Tite Laboise stood.

Charle', magnificent of inches, scorned his less-developed antagonist.

"Eh, man Gurdon," softly called old Robert Stuart from his window, "set them to it, will ye? The lads will be jawing till the morn's morn."

This equivocal order had little effect on the ordained course of a voyageur's quarrel.

"These St. Martins without stomachs, how is a man to hit them?—pouf!" said Charle', and Étienne felt on his tender spot the cruel allusion to his brother Alexis, whose stomach had been made public property. He began to shed tears of wrath.

"I will take your scalp for that! As for the black feather, I trample it under my foot!"

"Let me see you trample it. And my head is not so easily scalped as your brother's stomach."

All the time they were dancing around each other in graceful and menacing feints. But now they clinched, and Charle' Charette, when the struggle had lasted two or three minutes, took his antagonist like a puppy and flung him revolving to the ground. He hitched his belt and glanced up towards the sally-port as he stood back laughing.

Étienne was on foot with a tiger's bound. He had no chance with the wearer of the black feather, as everybody in the yard knew, and usually a beaten antagonist was ready to shake hands after a few trials of strength. But he seized one of the knives used in opening packs and struck at the victor's

side. As soon as he had struck and the bloody knife
came back in his hand he crouched and rolled his
eyes around in apology. No man was afraid of
shedding blood in those days, but he felt he had
gone too far—that his quarrel was not sufficiently
grounded. He heard a woman's scream, and the
sharp checking exclamation of his master, and felt
himself seized on each side. There was much confusion in his mind and in the yard, but he knew
'Tite Laboise flew through the gate and past him,
and he tried to propitiate her by a look.

"Pig!" she projected at him like a missile, and
he sat down on the ground between the guards who
were trying to hold him up and wept copiously.

"I didn't want to have trouble with that
Charle' Charette and that 'Tite Laboise," explained
Étienne. "And I don't want any black feather.
It was my brother's stomach. On account of my
brother's stomach I have to fight. If they do not
let my brother's stomach alone, I will have to kill
the whole brigade."

But Charle' Charette walked into the Fur Company's building feeling nothing but disdain for the
puny stock of St. Martin, as he held out his arm
and let the blood drip from a little wound that
stained his calico shirt-sleeve. The very neips
around his ankles seemed to tingle with desire to
kick poor Étienne.

It was not necessary to send for the surgeon of
the fort. Robert Stuart dressed the wound, salv-
ing it with the rebukes which he knew discipline

demanded, and making them as strong as his own enjoyment had been. He promised to break the head of every voyageur in the yard with a board if another quarrel occurred. And he pretended not to see the culprit's trembling wife, that little besom whose caprices had set the men by the ears ever since she was old enough to know the figures of a dance, yet for whom he and Mrs. Stuart had a warm corner in their hearts. She had caused the first fracas of the season, moreover. He went out and slammed the office door, ordering the men away from it.

"Bring me yon Étienne St. Martin," commanded Mr. Stuart, preparing his arsenal of strong language. "I'll have a word with yon carl for this."

The noise of the one-sided conflict could be heard in the office, but 'Tite remained as if she heard nothing, with her head and arms on the desk. Her husband took up the cap with the black feather, which he had thrown off in the presence of his superior. He rested it against his side, his elbow pointing a triangle, and waited aggressively for her to speak. The back of her pretty neck and fine tendrils of curly hair ruffled above it were very moving; but his heart swelled indignantly.

"'Tite Laboise, why did you shut the door in my face when I came back to you after a year's absence?"

She answered faintly, "Me, I don't know."

"And dance with Étienne St. Martin until I am obliged to whip him?"

"Me, I don't know."

"Yes, you do know. You have concealments," he accused, and she made no defence. "This is the case : you run to the dock to see the boats come in ; you are joyful until you watch me step ashore ; I look for 'Tite ; her back is disappearing at the corner of the street. Eh bien ! I say, she would rather meet me in the house. I fly to the house. My wife refuses to see me."

'Tite made no answer.

"What have I done ?" Charle' spread his hands. "My commandant has no complaint to make of me. It is Charle' Charette who leads on the trail or breaks a road where there is none, and carries the heaviest pack of furs, and pulls men out of the water when they are drowning ; it is Charle' Charette who can best endure fasting when the rations run low, and can hunt and bring in meat when other voyageurs lie exhausted about the camp-fire. I am no little lard-eater from Canada, brother to a man with a stomach having no lid. Look at that." Charle' shook the decorated cap at her. "I wear the black feather of my brigade. That means that I am the best man in it."

His wife reared her head. She was like the wild sweet-brier roses which crowded alluvial strips of the island, fragrant and pink and bristling. "Yes, monsieur, that black feather—regard it. Me, I am sick of that black feather. You say I have concealments. I have. All winter I go lonely. The ice is massed on the lake ; the snow is so deep, the wind is keener than a knife; I weep for my husband away in the wilderness, believing he thinks of me. Eh bien! he comes back to Mackinac. It is as you say: I fly to meet him, my breath chokes me. But my husband, what does he do?" She looked him up and down with wrathful eyes. " He does not see 'Tite. He sees nothing but that black feather in his cap that he must take off and show to Monsieur Ramsay Crooks and Monsieur Stuart —while his wife suffocates."

Charle' shrunk from his height, and his mouth opened like a fish's. " But I thought you would be proud of it."

" Me, what do I care how many men you have thrown down? You do not like me any better because you have thrown down all the men in your brigade."

" She is jealous—jealous of a feather!"

Humbled as he was by her tongue, the young voyageur felt delighted at giving his wife so trivial a rival.

He settled his belt and approached her and bowed. " Madame, permit me to offer you this black quill, which I have won for your sake, and which I boasted of to my masters that they might know you have not thrown yourself away on the poorest creature in Mackinac. Destroy it, madame. It was only the poor token of my love for you."

Graceful and polite as all the voyageurs were, Charle' Charette was the prince of them with his big sweet presence as he bent. 'Tite flew at him and flung her arms around his neck. After the manner of Latin peoples, they instantly shed tears upon each other, and the black feather was crushed between their breasts.

THE COBBLER IN THE DEVIL'S KITCHEN

EARLY in the Mackinac summer Owen Cunning took his shoemaker's bench and all his belongings to that open cavern on the beach called the Devil's Kitchen, which was said to derive its name from former practices of the Indians. They roasted prisoners there. The inner rock retained old smoke-stains.

Though appearing a mere hole in the cliff to passing canoe-men, the Devil's Kitchen was really as large as a small cabin, rising at least seven feet from a floor which sloped down towards the water. Overhead, through an opening which admitted his body, Owen could reach a natural attic, just large enough for his bed if he contented himself with blankets. And an Irishman prided himself on being tough as any French voyageur who slept blanketed on snow in the winter wilderness.

The rock was full of pockets, enclosing pebbles and fragments. By knocking out the contents of these, Owen made cupboards for his food. As for clothes, what Mackinac-Islander of the working-class, in those days of the Fur Company's prosperity, needed more than he had on? When his clothes wore out, Owen could go to the traders' and buy more. He washed his other shirt in the lake at his feet, and hung it on the cedars to dry by his door. Warm evenings, when the sun had soaked itself in limpid ripples until its crimson spread through them afar, Owen stripped himself and went bathing, with strong snorts of enjoyment as he rose from his plunge. The narrow lake rim was littered with fragments which had once filled the cavern. Two large pieces afforded him a table and a seat for his visitors.

Owen had a choice of water for his drinking. Not thirty feet away on his right a spring burst from the cliff and gushed through its little pool down the beach. It was cold and delicious.

In the east side of the Kitchen was a natural tiny fireplace a couple of feet high, screened by cedar foliage from the lake wind. Here Owen cooked his meals, and the smoke was generally carried out from his flueless hearth. The straits were then full of fish, and he had not far to throw his lines to reach deep water.

Dependent on the patronage of Mackinac village, the Irishman had chosen the very shop which would draw notice upon himself. His customers tramped out to him along a rough beach under the heights, which helped to wear away the foot-gear Owen mended. They stood grinning amiably at his snug quarters. It was told as far as Drummond Island

and the Sault that a cobbler lived in the Devil's Kitchen on Mackinac.

He was a happy fellow, his clean Irish skin growing rosier in air pure as the air of mid-ocean. The lake spread in variegated copper lights almost at his feet. He did not like Mackinac village in summer, when the engagés were all back, and Indians camped tribes strong on the beach, to receive their money from the government. French and savages shouldered one another, the multitude of them making a great hubbub and a gay show of clothes like a fair. Every voyageur was sparring with every other voyageur. A challenge by the poke of a fist, and lo! a ring is formed and two are fighting. The whipped one gets up, shakes hands with his conqueror, and off they go to drink together. Owen despised such fighting. His way was to take a club and break heads, and see some blood run on the ground. It was better for him to dwell alone than to be stirred up and left unsatisfied.

It was late in the afternoon, and the fresh smell of the water cheered him as he sat stitching on a pair of deer-hide shoes for one Léon Baudette, an engagé, who was homesick for Montreal. The lowering sun smote an hour-glass of light across the strait which separated him from St. Ignace on the north shore, the old Jesuit station. Mother-of-pearl clouds hung over the southern mainland, and the wash of the lake, which was as pleasant as silence itself, diverted his mind from a distant thump of Indian drums. He knew how lazy, naked warriors lay in their lodges, bumping a mallet on stretched deer-hide and droning barbarous mono-tones while they kicked their heels in air. If he despised anything more than the way the French diverted themselves, it was the way the Indians diverted themselves.

Without a sound there came into Owen's view on the right an Indian girl. He was at first taken by surprise at her coming over the moss of the spring. The shaggy cliff, clothed, like the top of his cave, with cedars, white birch, and pine, afforded no path to the beach in that direction. All his clients approached by the lake margin at the left.

Then he noticed it was Blackbird, a Sac girl, who had been pointed out to his critical eye the previous summer as a beauty. Owen admitted she was not bad-looking for a squaw. Her burnished hair, which had got her the name, was drawn down to cheeks where copper and vermilion infused the skin with a wonderful sunset tint. She was neatly and precisely dressed in the woman's skirt and jacket of her tribe, even her moccasins showing no trace of the scramble she must have had down some secret cliff descent in order to approach the cob-bler unseen.

He greeted her with the contemptuous affability which an Irishman bestows upon a heathen. Black-bird was probably a good communicant of some wilderness mission, but this brought her no nearer to a son of Ireland.

"Good-day to the quane! And what may she be wanting the day?"

Blackbird's eyes, without the snake-restlessness of her race, dwelt unmoving upon him. Owen surmised she could not understand his or any other kind of English, being accustomed to no tongue but her own, except the French which the engagés talked in their winter camps. She stood upright as a pine without answering.

It flashed through him that there might be trouble in the village; and Blackbird, having regard for him, as we think it possible any human being may have for us, was there to bid him escape. With coldness around the roots of his hair, he remembered the massacre at Fort Michilimackinac—a spot almost in sight across the strait, where south shore approaches north shore at the mouth of Lake Michigan. He laid down his boot. His lips dropped apart, and with a hush of the sound—if such a sound can be hushed—he imitated the Indian war-whoop.

Blackbird did not smile at the uncanny screech, but she relaxed her face in stoic amusement, relieving Owen's tense breathing. There was no plot. The tribes merely intended to draw their money, get as drunk as possible, and depart in peace at the end of the month with various outfits to winter posts.

"Begorra, but that was a narrow escape!" sighed Owen, wiping his forehead on his sleeve. He was able to detect the deference that Blackbird paid him by this visit. He sat on his bench in the

38

Kitchen, a sunny idol in a shrine, indifferent to the effect his background gave him.

His mouth puckered. He put up his leather stained hand coyly, and motioned her unmoving figure back.

"Ah, go 'way! Wasn't it to escape you and the likes of you that I made me retrate to the shore? Nayther white, full haythen, half, nor quarther nade apply. To come makin' the big eyes at me, and the post swarmin' wid thim that do be ready to marry on any woman at the droppin' of the hat!"

Mobile blue water with ripple and wash made a background for the Indian girl's dense repose. She could by lifting her eyes see the pock-marked front of Owen's Kitchen, and gnarled roots like exposed ribs in the shaggy heights above. But she kept her eyes lowered; and Owen stuck his feet under his bench, sensitive to defects in his foot-wear, which an artist skilled in making and mending moccasins could detect.

Blackbird moved forward and laid a shining dot on the stone he used as his table; then, without a word, she turned and disappeared the way she came, over the moss of the spring rivulet.

Owen left his bench and craned after her. He did not hear a pebble roll on the stony beach or a twig snap among foliage.

"Begorra, it's the wings of a say-gull!" said Owen, and he took up her offering. It was a tiny gold coin. Mackinac was full of gold the month the Indians were paid. It came in kegs from

Washington, under the escort of soldiers, to the United States Agency, and was weighed out to each red heir despoiled of land by white conquest, in his due proportion, and immediately grasped from the improvident by merchants, for a little pork, a little whiskey, a little calico. But this was an old coin with a hole in it; a jewel worn suspended from neck or ear; the precious trinket of a girl. On one side was rudely scratched the outline of a bird.

"Begorra!" said Owen. He hid it in one of the rock pockets, a trust in a savings-bank, and sat down again to work, trying to discover Blackbird's object in offering tribute to him.

About sunset he lighted a fire in his low grate to cook his supper, and put the finished boots in a remote corner of the cave until he should get his pay. As he expected, Léon Baudette appeared, picking a barefooted way along the beach, with many complimentary greetings. The wary cobbler stood between the boots and his client, and responded with open cordiality. A voyageur who gave flesh and bone and sometimes life itself for a hundred dollars a year, and drank that hundred dollars up during his month of semi-civilization on Mackinac, seldom had much about him with which to pay for his necessary mending.

Léon Baudette swore at the price, being a discontented engagé. But the foot-wear he was obliged to have, being secretly determined to desert to Canada before the boats went out. You may see his name marked as a deserter in the Fur Company's

40

books at Mackinac Island. So, reluctantly counting out the money, he put on his shoes and crossed his legs to smoke and chat, occupying the visitor's seat. Owen put his kettle to boil, and sat down also to enjoy society; for why should man be hurried?

He learned how many fights had been fought that day; how many bales of furs were packed in the Company's yard; that Étienne St. Martin was trying to ship with the Northern instead of the Illinois Brigade, on account of a grudge against Charle' Charette. He learned that the Indians were having snake and medicine dances to cure a consumptive chief. And, to his surprise, he learned that he was considered a medicine-man among the tribes, on account of his living unmolested in the Devil's Kitchen.

"O oui," declared Léon. "You de wizard. You only play you mend de shoe; but, by gar, you make de poor voyageur pay de same like it was work! I hear dey call you Big Medicine of de Cuisine Diable."

Owen was compelled to smile with pleasure at his importance, his long upper lip lifting its unshaven bristles in a white curd.

"Do ye moind, Leen me boy, a haythen Injun lady by the name of Blackbird?"

"Me, I know Blackbird," responded Léon Baudette.

"Is the consoompted chafe that they're makin' the snake shindy for married on her?"

"No, no. Blackbird she wife of Jean Magliss in de winter camps."

" John McGillis?   Is it for marryin' on a haythen wife he is?"

" O oui. Two wives. One good Cat'olique. Jean Magliss, he dance every night now with Amable Morin's girl. The more weddings, the more dancing. Me," Léon shrugged, " I no want a woman eating my wages in Mackinac. A squaw in the winter camps—'t assez."

" Two wives, the bog-trotter!" gulped Owen. " John McGillis is a blayguard!"

" Oui, what you call Irish," assented Léon ; and he dodged, but the cobbler threw nothing at him. Owen marked with the awl on his own leather apron.

" First a haythen and then a quarther-brade," he tallied against his countryman.   " He will be takin' his quarther-brade to the praste before the boats go out?"

Léon raised fat eyebrows. " Amable Morin, he no fool. It is six daughters he has. O oui; the marriage is soon made."   '

" And the poor haythen, what does she do now?"

" Blackbird? She watch Jean Magliss dance. Then she leave her lodge and take to de pine wood. Blackbird ver fond of what you call de Irish."

Owen was little richer in the gift of expression than the Indian woman, but he could feel the tragedy of her unconfirmed marriage. A squaw was taken to her lord's wigwam, and remained as long as she pleased him. He could divorce her with a gift, proportioned to his means and her worth.

When Léon Baudette departed, Owen prepared and ate his supper, brewing himself some herb tea and seasoning it with a drop of whiskey.

The evening beauty of the lake, of coasts melting in general dimness, and that iridescent stony hook stretched out from Round Island to grapple passing craft, was lost on Owen. Humid air did not soften the glower which grew and hardened on his visage as he made his preparations for night. These were very simple. The coals of drift-wood soon died to white ashes in his grate. To close the shop was to stand upon the shoemaker's bench and reach for the ladder in his attic—a short ladder that just performed its office and could be hidden aloft.

Drawing his stairway after him when he had ascended, Owen spread and arranged his blankets. The ghosts that rose from tortured bodies in the Kitchen below never worked any terror in his imagination when he went to bed. Rather, he lay stretched in his hard cradle gloating over the stars, his wild security, the thousand night aspects of nature which he could make part of himself without expressing. For him the moon cast gorgeous bridges on the water; the breathing of the woods was the breathing of a colossal brother; and when that awful chill which precedes the resurrection of day rose from the earth and started from the rock, he turned comfortably in his thick bedding and taxed sleepy eyes to catch the wanness coming over the lake.

But instead of lying down in his usual peace

when the nest was made to suit him, Owen wheeled
and hung undecided legs over the edge of his loft.
Then he again put down the ladder and descended.
He had trod the three-quarters of a mile of beach
to the village but once since the boats came in.
Now that his mind was fixed he took to it again
with a loping step, bending his body forward and
grasping his cap to butt through trailing foliage.

As he passed the point and neared the post, its
blare and hubbub burst on him, and its torch-light
and many twinkling candles. He proceeded beside
the triple row of Indian lodges which occupied the
entire water-front. At intervals, on the very verge,
evening fires were built, throwing streamers of
crimson flicker on the lake. Naked pappooses
gathered around these at play. But on an open flat
betwixt encampment and village rose a lighted
tabernacle of blankets stretched on poles and uprights; and within this the adult Indians were
crowded, celebrating the orgy of the medicine-dance.
Their noise kept a continuous roll of echoes moving
across the islands.

Owen made haste to pass this carnival of invocation
and plunge into the swarming main street of Mackinac, where a thousand voyageurs roved, ready to
embrace any man and call him brother and press
him to drink with them. Broad low houses with
huge chimney-stacks and dormer-windows stood
open and hospitable; for Mackinac was en fête
while the fur season lasted. One huge storage-room,
a wing of the Fur Company's building, was lighted

44

with candles around the sides for the nightly ball. Squared dark joists of timber showed overhead. The fiddlers sat on a raised platform, playing in ecstasy. The dark, shining floor was thronged with dancers, who, before primrose-color entirely withdrew from evening twilight, had rushed to their usual amusement. Half-breeds, quarter-breeds, sixteenth-breeds, Canadian French, Americans, in finery that the Northwest was able to command from marts of the world, crossed, joined hands, and whirled, the rhythmic tread of feet sounding like the beating of a great pulse. The doors of double timber stood open. From where he paused outside, Owen could see mighty hinges stretching across the whole width of these doors.

And he could see John McGillis moving among the most agile dancers. When at last the music stopped, and John led Amable Morin's girl to one of the benches along the wall, Owen was conscious that an Indian woman crossed the lighted space behind him, and he turned and looked full at Blackbird, and she looked full at him. But she did not stay to be included in the greeting of John McGillis, though English might be better known to her than Owen had supposed.

John came heartily to the door and endeavored to pull his countryman in. He was a much younger man than Owen, a handsome, light-haired voyageur, with thick eyelids and cajoling blue eyes. John was the only Irish engagé in the brigades. The sweet gift of blarney dwelt on his broad red lips.

He looked too amiable and easily entreated, too much in love with life, indeed, to quarrel with any one. Yet as Owen answered his invitation by a quick pass that struck his cheek, his color mounted with zest, and he stepped out, turning up his sleeves.

"Is it a foight ye want, ye old wizard from the Divil's Kitchen?" laughed John, still good-natured.

"It's a foight I want," responded Owen. "It's a foight I'm shpilin' for. Come out forninst the place, where the shlobberin' Frinch can lave a man be, and I'll shpake me moind."

John walked bareheaded with him, and they passed around the building to a fence enclosing the Fur Company's silent yard. Stockades of sharp-pointed cedar posts outlined gardens near them. A smell of fur mingled with odors of sweetbrier and loam. Again the violins excited that throb of dancing feet, and John McGillis moved his arms in time to the music.

"Out wid it, Owen. I'm losin' me shport."

"John McGillis, are ye not own cousin to me by raisin of marryin' on as fine a colleen as iver shtepped in Ireland?"

"I am, Owen, I am."

"Did ye lave that same in sorrow, consatin' to fetch her out to Ameriky whin yer fortune was made?"

"I did, Owen, I did."

"Whin ye got word of her death last year, was ye a broken-hearted widdy or was ye not?"

"I was, Owen, I was."

46

"John McGillis, do ye call yerself a widdy now, or do ye not call yerself a widdy?"

"I do, Owen, I do."

"Thin ye're the loire," and Owen slapped his face.

For a minute there was danger of manslaughter as they dealt each other blows with sledge fists. Instead of clinching, they stood apart and cudgelled fiercely with the knuckled hand. The first round ended in blood, which John wiped from his face with a new bandanna, and Owen flung contemptuously from his nose with finger and thumb. The lax-muscled cobbler was no match for the fresh and vigorous voyageur, and he knew it, but went stubbornly to work again, saying, grimly:

"I've shpiled yer face for the gu'urls the night, bedad."

They pounded each other without mercy, and again rested, Owen this time leaning against the fence to breathe.

"John McGillis, are ye a widdy or are ye not a widdy?" he challenged, as soon as he could speak.

"I am, Owen Cunnin', I am," maintained John.

"Thin I repate ye're the loire!" And once more they came to the proof, until Owen lay upon the ground kicking to keep his opponent off.

"Will I bring ye the dhrop of whiskey, Owen?" suggested John, tenderly.

His cousin by marriage crawled to the fence and sat up, without replying.

"I've the flask in me pouch, Owen."

"Kape it there."

"But sure if ye foight wid me ye'll dhrink wid me?"

"I'll not dhrink a dhrop wid ye."

The cobbler panted heavily. "The loikes of you that do be goin' to marry on a Frinch quarther-brade, desavin' her, and the father and the mother and the praste, that you do be a widdy."

"I am a widdy, Owen."

The cobbler made a feint to rise, but sank back, repeating, at the top of his breath, "Ye're the loire!"

"What do ye mane?" sternly demanded John. "Ye know I've had me throuble. Ye know I've lost me wife in the old counthry. It's a year gone. Was the praste that wrote the letther a loire?"

"I have a towken that ye're not the widdy ye think ye are."

John came to Owen and stooped over him, grasping him by the collar. Candle-light across the street and stars in a steel-blue sky did not reveal faces distinctly, but his shaking of the cobbler was an outcome of his own inward convulsion. He belonged to a class in whom memory and imagination were not strong, being continually taxed by a present of large action crowded with changing images. But when his past rose up it took entire possession of him.

"Why didn't ye tell me this before?"

"I've not knowed it the long time meself."

"What towken have ye got?"

"Towken enough for you and me."

"Show it to me."

"I will not."

"Ye're desavin' me. Ye have no towken."

"Thin marry on yer quarther-brade if ye dare!"

To be unsettled and uninterested in his surroundings was John McGillis's portion during the remaining weeks of his stay on the island. Half savage and half tender he sat in his barracks and smoked large pipes of tobacco.

He tramped out nearly every evening to the Devil's Kitchen, and had wordy battles, which a Frenchman would have called fights, with the cobbler, though the conferences always ended by his producing his ration and supping and smoking there. He coaxed his cousin to show him the token, vacillating between hope of impossible news from a wife he had every reason to believe dead, and indignation at being made the sport of Owen's stubbornness. Learning in the Fur Company's office that Owen had received news from the old country in the latest mail sent out of New York, he was beside himself, and Amable Morin's girl was forgotten. He began to believe he had never thought of her.

"Sure, the old man Morin and me had some words and a dhrink over it, was all. I did but dance wid her and pinch her cheek. A man niver knows what he does on Mackinac till he comes to himself in the winter camps wid a large family on his moind."

"The blarney of your lip doesn't desave me, John McGillis," responded his cousin the cobbler, with grimness.

"But whin will ye give me the word you've got, Owen?"

"I'll not give it to ye till the boats go out."

"Will ye tell me, is the colleen alive, thin?"

"I've tould ye ye're not a widdy."

"If the colleen is alive, the towken would be sint to me."

"Thin ye've got it," said Owen.

Poor John smoked, biting hard on his pipe-stem. Ignorance, and the helplessness of a limited man who is more a good animal than a discerning soul; time, the slow transmission of news, his fixed state as a voyageur—all these things were against him. He could not adjust himself to any facts, and his feelings sometimes approached the melting state. It was no use to war with Owen Cunning, whom he was ashamed of handling roughly. The cobbler sat with swollen and bandaged face, talking out of a slit, still bullying him.

But the time came for his brigade to go out, and then there was action, decision, positive life once more. It went far northward, and was first to depart, in order to reach winter-quarters before snow should fly.

At the log dock the boats waited, twelve of them in this outfit, each one a mighty Argo, rowed by a dozen pairs of oars, and with centre-piece for stepping a mast. Hundreds of pounds they could carry, and a crew of fifteen men. The tarpaulin used for a night covering and to shelter the trading-goods from storms was large as the roof of a house.

Quiescent on lapping water they rested, their loads and each man's baggage of twenty or fewer pounds packed tightly to place.

The cobbler from the Devil's Kitchen was in the crowd thronging dock and shore. The villagers were there, saying farewells, and all the voyageurs who were soon to go out in other brigades snuffed as war-horses ready for the charge. The life of the woods, which was their true life, again drew them. They could scarcely wait. Dancing and love-making suddenly cloyed; for a man was made to conquer the wilderness and take the spoils of the earth. Woodsman's habits returned upon them. The frippery of the island was dropped like the withes which bound Samson. Their companions the Indians were also making ready the canoes. Blackbird stood erect behind the elbow of John McGillis as he took leave of his cousin the cobbler.

"Do ye moind, Owen," exclaimed John, turning from the interests of active life to that which had disturbed his spirit, convinced unalterably of his own widowed state, yet harrowed unspeakably, "ye promised to show me that word from the old counthry before the boats wint out."

"I niver promised to show ye any word from the old counthry," responded Owen, having his mouth free of bandages and both eyes for the boats.

"Ye tould me ye had a towken from the old counthry."

"I niver tould ye I had a towken from the old counthry."

"Ye did tell me ye had a towken."

"I have."

"Ye said it proved I was not a widdy."

"I did."

"Show me that same, thin."

"I will."

Owen looked steadily past John's shoulder at Blackbird, and laid in John's hand a small gold coin with a hole in it, on one side of which was rudely scratched the outline of a bird.

John McGillis's face burned red, and many expressions besides laughter crossed it. Like a child detected in fault, he looked sheepishly at Owen and glanced behind his shoulder. The faithful sunset-tinted face of Blackbird, immovable as a fixed star, regarded the battered cobbler as it might have regarded a great manitou when the island was young.

"How did you come by this, Owen?"

"I come by it from one that had throuble. Has yerself iver seen it before, John McGillis?"

"I have."

"Is it a towken that ye're not a widdy?"

"It is."

The boats went out, and Blackbird sat in her Irish husband's boat, on his baggage. Oars flashed, and the commandant's boat led the way. Then the life of the Northwest rose like a great wave—the voyageurs' song chanted by a hundred and fifty throats, with a chorus of thousands on the shore:

Dans les chan-tiers nous hi - ver - ne - rons!

Dans les chan-tiers nous hi - ver - ne - rons!

When Owen returned to his Kitchen he found a robe of the finest beaver folded and laid on his shoemaker's bench.

"Begorra!" observed the cobbler, shaking it out and rubbing it against his cheek, "she has paid me a beaver-shkin and the spalpeen wasn't worrth it. But she can kape him now till she has a moind to turn him out herself. Whin a man marries on a haythen, wid praste or widout praste, let him shtick to his haythen."

THE SKELETON ON ROUND ISLAND

On the 15th day of March, 1897, Ignace Pelott died at Mack-
inac Island, aged ninety-three years.

The old quarter-breed, son of a half-breed Chippewa mother and
French father, took with him into silence much wilderness lore of
the Northwest. He was full of stories when warmed to recital,
though at the beginning of a talk his gentle eyes dwelt on the listener
with anxiety, and he tapped his forehead—" So many things gone
from there!" His habit of saying " Oh God, yes," or " Oh God,
no," was not in the least irreverent, but simply his mild way of
using island English.

While water lapped the beach before his door and the sun smote
sparkles on the strait, he told about this adventure across the ice,
and his hearer has taken but few liberties with the recital.

I AM to carry Mamselle Rosalin of Green Bay
from Mackinac to Cheboygan that time, and
it is the end of March, and the wind have turn
from east to west in the morning. A man will go
out with the wind in the east, to haul wood from
Boblo, or cut a hole to fish, and by night he cannot
get home—ice, it is rotten; it goes to pieces quick
when the March wind turns.

I am not afraid for me—long, tall fellow then;
eye that can see to Point aux Pins; I can lift more

than any other man that goes in the boats to Green
Bay or the Soo; can swim, run on snow-shoes, go
without eating two, three days, and draw my belt
in. Sometimes the ice-floes carry me miles, for they
all go east down the lakes when they start, and I
have landed the other side of Drummond. But
when you have a woman with you—Oh God, yes,
that is different.

The way of it is this: I have brought the mail
from St. Ignace with my traino — you know the
train-au-galise—the birch sledge with dogs. It is
flat, and turn up at the front like a toboggan. And
I have take the traino because it is not safe for a
horse; the wind is in the west, and the strait bends
and looks too sleek. Ice a couple of inches thick will
bear up a man and dogs. But this old ice a foot
thick, it is turning rotten. I have come from St.
Ignace early in the afternoon, and the people crowd
about to get their letters, and there is Mamselle
Rosalin crying to go to Cheboygan, because her
lady has arrive there sick, and has sent the letter a
week ago. Her friends say:

"It is too late to go to-day, and the strait is
dangerous."

She say: "I make a bundle and walk. I must
go when my lady is sick and her husband the lieutenant is away, and she has need of me."

Mamselle's friends talk and she cry. She runs
and makes a little bundle in the house and comes
out ready to walk to Cheboygan. There is nobody
can prevent her. Some island people are descend

from noblesse of France. But none of them have travel like Mamselle Rosalin with the officer's wife to Indiana, to Chicago, to Detroit. She is like me, French.* The girls use to turn their heads to see me walk in to mass; but I never look grand as Mamselle Rosalin when she step out to that ice.

I have not a bit of sense; I forget maman and my brothers and sisters that depend on me. I run to Mamselle Rosalin, take off my cap, and bow from my head to my heel, like you do in the dance. I will take her to Cheboygan with my traino—Oh God, yes! And I laugh at the wet track the sledge make, and pat my dogs and tell them they are not tired. I wrap her up in the fur, and she thank me and tremble, and look me through with her big black eyes so that I am ready to go down in the strait.

The people on the shore hurrah, though some of them cry out to warn us.

"The ice is cracked from Mission Point to the hook of Round Island, Ignace Pelott!"

"I know that," I say. "Good-day, messieurs!"

The crack from Mission Point—under what you call Robinson's Folly—to the hook of Round Island always comes first in a breaking up; and I hold my breath in my teeth as I skurry the dogs across it. The ice grinds, the water follows the sledge. But the sun is so far down in the southwest, I think "The wind will grow colder. The real thaw will not come before to-morrow."

* The old fellow would not own the Chippewa.

THE TRAIN-AU-GALISE

I am to steer betwixt the east side of Round Island and Boblo. When we come into the shadow of Boblo we are chill with damp, far worse than the clear sharp air that blows from Canada. I lope beside the traino, and not take my eyes off the course to Cheboygan, except that I see the islands look blue, and darkness stretching before its time. The sweat drop off my face, yet I feel that wind through my wool clothes, and am glad of the shelter between Boblo and Round Island, for the strait outside will be the worst.

There is an Indian burying-ground on open land above the beach on that side of Round Island. I look up when the thick woods are pass, for the sunset ought to show there. But what I see is a skeleton like it is sliding down hill from the graveyard to the beach. It does not move. The earth is wash from it, and it hangs staring at me.

I cannot tell how that make me feel! I laugh, for it is funny; but I am ashame, like my father is expose and Mamselle Rosalin can see him. If I do not cover him again I am disgrace. I think I will wait till some other day when I can get back from Cheboygan; for what will she say if I stop the traino when we have such a long journey, and it is so near night, and the strait almost ready to move? So I crack the whip, but something pull, pull! I cannot go on! I say to myself, " The ground is froze; how can I cover up that skeleton without any shovel, or even a hatchet to break the earth?"

But something pull, pull, so I am oblige to stop,

and the dogs turn in without one word and drag
the sledge up the beach of Round Island.

"What is the matter?" says Mamselle Rosalin.
She is out of the sledge as soon as it stops.

I not know what to answer, but tell her I have
to cut a stick to mend my whip-handle. I think I
will cut a stick and rake some earth over the skeleton to cover it, and come another day with a shovel
and dig a new grave. The dogs lie down and pant,
and she looks through me with her big eyes like
she beg me to hurry.

But there is no danger she will see the skeleton.
We both look back to Mackinac. The island have
its hump up against the north, and the village in its
lap around the bay, and the Mission eastward near
the cliff; but all seem to be moving! We run along
the beach of Round Island, and then we see the
channel between that and Boblo is moving too, and
the ice is like wet loaf-sugar, grinding as it floats.

We hear some roars away off, like cannon when
the Americans come to the island. My head swims.
I cross myself and know why something pull, pull,
to make me bring the traino to the beach, and I am
oblige to that skeleton who slide down hill to warn
me.

When we have seen Mackinac, we walk to the
other side and look south and southeast towards
Cheboygan. All is the same. The ice is moving
out of the strait.

"We are strand on this island!" says Mamselle
Rosalin. "Oh, what shall we do?"

I tell her it is better to be prisoners on Round Island than on a cake of ice in the strait, for I have tried the cake of ice and know.

"We will camp and build a fire in the cove opposite Mackinac," I say. "Maman and the children will see the light and feel sure we are safe."

"I have done wrong," says she. "If you lose your life on this journey, it is my fault."

Oh God, no! I tell her. She is not to blame for anything, and there is no danger. I have float many a time when the strait breaks up, and not save my hide so dry as it is now. We only have to stay on Round Island till we can get off.

"And how long will that be?" she ask.

I shrug my shoulders. There is no telling. Sometimes the strait clears very soon, sometimes not. Maybe two, three days.

Rosalin sit down on a stone.

I tell her we can make camp, and show signals to Mackinac, and when the ice permit, a boat will be sent.

She is crying, and I say her lady will be well. No use to go to Cheboygan anyhow, for it is a week since her lady sent for her. But she cry on, and I think she wish I leave her alone, so I say I will get wood. And I unharness the dogs, and run along the beach to cover that skeleton before dark. I look and cannot find him at all. Then I go up to the graveyard and look down. There is no skeleton anywhere. I have seen his skull and his ribs and his arms and legs, all sliding down hill. But he is gone!

The dusk close in upon the islands, and I not know what to think—cross myself, two, three times; and wish we had land on Boblo instead of Round Island, though there are wild beasts on both.

But there is no time to be scare at skeletons that slide down and disappear, for Mamselle Rosalin must have her camp and her place to sleep. Every man use to the bateaux have always his tinder-box, his knife, his tobacco, but I have more than that; I have leave Mackinac so quick I forget to take out the storekeeper's bacon that line the bottom of the sledge, and Mamselle Rosalin sit on it in the furs! We have plenty meat, and I sing like a voyageur while I build the fire. Drift, so dry in summer you can light it with a coal from your pipe, lay on the beach, but is now winter-soaked, and I make a fire-place of logs, and cut pine branches to help it.

It is all thick woods on Round Island, so close it tear you to pieces if you try to break through; only four-footed things can crawl there. When the fire is blazing up I take my knife and cut a tunnel like a little room, and pile plenty evergreen branches. This is to shelter Mamselle Rosalin, for the night is so raw she shiver. Our tent is the sky, darkness, and clouds. But I am happy. I unload the sledge. The bacon is wet. On long sticks the slices sizzle and sing while I toast them, and the dogs come close and blink by the fire, and lick their chops. Rosalin laugh and I laugh, for it smell like a good kitchen;

"'I THINK THE CAMP GO AROUND AND AROUND ME'"

and we sit and eat nothing but toasted meat—better than lye corn and tallow that you have when you go out with the boats. Then I feed the dogs, and she walk with me to the water edge, and we drink with our hands.

It is my house, when we sit on the fur by the fire. I am so light I want my fiddle. I wish it last like a dream that Mamselle Rosalin and me keep house together on Round Island. You not want to go to heaven when the one you think about all the time stays close by you.

But pretty soon I want to go to heaven quick. I think I jump in the lake if maman and the children had anybody but me. When I light my pipe she smile. Then her great big eyes look off towards Mackinac, and I turn and see the little far-away lights.

"They know we are on Round Island together," I say to cheer her, and she move to the edge of the fur. Then she say "Good-night," and get up and go to her tunnel-house in the bushes, and I jump up too, and spread the fur there for her. And I not get back to the fire before she make a door of all the branches I have cut, and is hid like a squirrel. I feel I dance for joy because she is in my camp for me to guard. But what is that? It is a woman that cry out loud by herself! I understand now why she sit down so hopeless when we first land. I have not know much about women, but I understand how she feel. It is not her lady, or the dark, or the ice break up, or the cold. It is not Ignace

Pelott. It is the name of being prison on Round Island with a man till the ice is out of the straits. She is so shame she want to die. I think I will kill myself. If Mamselle Rosalin cry out loud once more, I plunge in the lake—and then what become of maman and the children?

She is quieter; and I sit down and cannot smoke, and the dogs pity me. Old Sauvage lay his nose on my knee. I do not say a word to him, but I pat him, and we talk with our eyes, and the bright camp-fire shows each what the other is say.

"Old Sauvage," I tell him, "I am not good man like the priest. I have been out with the boats, and in Indian camps, and I not had in my life a chance to marry, because there are maman and the children. But you know, old Sauvage, how I have feel about Mamselle Rosalin, it is three years."

Old Sauvage hit his tail on the ground and answer he know.

"I have love her like a dog that not dare to lick her hand. And now she hate me because I am shut on Round Island with her while the ice goes out. I not good man, but it pretty tough to stand that."

Old Sauvage hit his tail on the ground and say, "That so." I hear the water on the gravel like it sound when we find a place to drink; then it is plenty company, but now it is lonesome. The water say to people on Mackinac, "Rosalin and Ignace Pelott, they are on Round Island." What make you proud, maybe, when you turn it and look at it the other way, make you sick. But I cannot walk the broken ice, and if I could, she would be lef alone with the dogs. I think I will build another camp.

But soon there is a shaking in the bushes, and Sauvage and his sledgemates bristle and stand up and show their teeth. Out comes Mamselle Rosalin with a scream to the other side of the fire.

I have nothing except my knife, and I take a chunk of burning wood and go into her house. Maybe I see some green eyes. I have handle vild-cat skin too much not to know that smell in the dark.

I take all the branches from Rosalin's house and pile them by the fire, and spread the fur robe on them. And I pull out red coals and put more logs on before I sit down away off between her and the spot where she hear that noise. If the graveyard was over us, I would expect to see that skeleton once more.

"What was it?" she whisper.

I tell her maybe a stray wolf.

"Wolves not eat people, mamselle, unless they hunt in a pack ; and they run from fire. You know what M'sieu' Cable tell about wolves that chase him on the ice when he skate to Cheboygan? He come to great wide crack in ice, he so scare he jump it and skate right on! Then he look back, and see the wolves go in, head down, every wolf caught and drown in the crack. It is two days before he come home, and the east wind have blow to freeze that crack over—and there are all the wolf tails, stick up, froze stiff in a row! He bring them home with him

—but los them on the way, though he show the knife that cut them off!"

"I have hear that," says Rosalin. "I think he lie."

"He say he take his oat on a book," I tell her, but we both laugh, and she is curl down so close to the fire her cheeks turn rosy. For a camp-fire will heat the air all around until the world is like a big dark room; and we are shelter from the wind. I am glad she is begin to enjoy herself. And all the time I have a hand on my knife, and the cold chills down my back where that hungry vild-cat will set his claws if he jump on me; and I cannot turn around to face him because Rosalin thinks it is nothing but a cowardly wolf that sneak away. Old Sauvage is uneasy and come to me, his fangs all expose, but I drive him back and listen to the bushes behind me.

"Sing, M'sieu' Pelott," says Rosalin.

Oh God, yes! it is easy to sing with a vild-cat watch you on one side and a woman on the other!

"But I not know anything except boat songs."

"Sing boat songs."

So I sing like a bateau full of voyageurs, and the dark echo, and that vild-cat must be astonish. When you not care what become of you, and your head is light and your heart like a stone on the beach, you not mind vild-cats, but sing and laugh.

I cast my eye behin sometimes, and feel my knife. It make me smile to think what kind of creature come to my house in the wilderness, and I say to myself: "Hear my cat purr! This is the only time

I will ever have a home of my own, and the only time the woman I want sit beside my fire."

Then I ask Rosalin to sing to me, and she sing "Malbrouck," like her father learn it in Kebec. She watch me, and I know her eyes have more danger for me than the vild-cat's. It ought to tear me to pieces if I forget maman and the children. It ought to be scare out the bushes to jump on a poor fool like me. But I not stop entertain it—Oh God, no! I say things that I never intend to say, like they are pull out of my mouth. When your heart has ache, sometimes it break up quick like the ice.

"There is Paul Pepin," I tell her. "He is a happy man; he not trouble himself with anybody at all. His father die; he let his mother take care of herself. He marry a wife, and get tired of her and turn her off with two children. The priest not able to scare him; he smoke and take his dram and enjoy life. If I was Paul Pepin I would not be torment."

"But you are not torment," says Rosalin. "Everybody speak well of you."

"Oh God, yes," I tell her; "but a man not live on the breath of his neighbors. I am thirty years old, and I have take care of my mother and brothers and sisters since I am fifteen. I not made so I can leave them, like Paul Pepin. He marry when he please. I not able to marry at all. It is not far I can go from the island. I cannot get rich. My work must be always the same."

"But why you want to marry?" says Rosalin, as if that surprise her. And I tell her it is because I have seen Rosalin of Green Bay; and she laugh. Then I think it is time for the vild-cat to jump. I am thirty years old, and have nothing but what I can make with the boats or my traino; the children are not grown; my mother depend on me; and I have propose to a woman, and she laugh at me!

But I not see, while we sing and talk, that the fire is burn lower, and old Sauvage has crept around the camp into the bushes.

That end all my courtship. I not use to it, and not have any business to court, anyhow. I drop my head on my breast, and it is like when I am little and the measle go in. Paul Pepin he take a woman by the chin and smack her on the lips., The women not laugh at him, he is so rough. I am as strong as he is, but I am afraid to hurt; I am oblige to take care of what need me. And I am tie to things I love — even the island — so that I cannot get away.

"I not want to marry," says Rosalin, and I see her shake her head at me. "I not think about it at all."

"Mamselle," I say to her, "you have not any inducement like I have, that torment you three years."

"How you know that?" she ask me. And then her face change from laughter, and she spring up from the blanket couch, and I think the camp go around and around me—all fur and eyes and claws and teeth — and I not know what I am doing, for the dogs are all over me—yell—yell—yell; and then I am stop stabbing, because the vild-cat has let go of Sauvage, and Sauvage has let go of the vild-cat, and I am looking at them and know they are both dead, and I cannot help him any more.

You are confuse by such things where there is noise, and howling creatures sit up and put their noses in the air, like they call their mate back out of the dark. I am sick for my old dog. Then I am proud he has kill it, and wipe my knife on its fur, but feel ashame that I have not check him driving it into camp. And then Rosalin throw her arms around my neck and kiss me.

It is many years I have tell Rosalin she did that. But a woman will deny what she know to be the trut. I have tell her the courtship had end, and she begin it again herself, and keep it up till the boats take us off Round Island. The ice not run out so quick any more now like it did then. My wife say it is a long time we waited, but when I look back it seem the shortest time I ever live—only two days.

Oh God, yes, it is three years before I marry the woman that not want to marry at all; then my brothers and sisters can take care of themselves, and she help me take care of maman.

It is when my boy Gabriel come home from the war to die that I see the skeleton on Round Island again. I am again sure it is wash out, and I go ashore to bury it, and it disappear. Nobody but me see it. Then before Rosalin die I am out on the ice-boat, and it give me warning. I know what it mean; but you cannot always escape misfortune. I cross myself when I see it; but I find good luck that first time I land; and maybe I find good luck every time, after I have land.

THE PENITENT OF CROSS VILLAGE

THE cross cast its shadow around its feet, so high noon stood over Cross Village. It was behind the church, rising above the gable, of silver-colored wood stained by weather to an almost phosphorescent glint. Seen from the lake the cross towered the most conspicuous thing on the bluff. A whitewashed fence stretched between it and the cliff, and on this fence sat Moses Nazagebic, looking across Lake Michigan.

He heard a soft tap on the ground near him and knew that his wife's grandmother had come out to walk there. She was the only villager, except his wife, whose approach he could endure. His wife stood some distance apart, protecting him, as Miriam protected the first Moses. Other women, gathered in the grove along the bluff to spread the festival mid-day meal, said to one another:

"Moses has now mourned a week for Frank Chibam and his shipwrecked boat and the white men. We shall miss Lucy's fish-pie this year."

"It was at last year's festival that Frank began

to notice Catharine. They were like one family, those four and the grandmother, especially after Moses and Frank bought the sail-boat together. No wonder the poor fellow sits on the fence and says nothing while the tribes are racing horses."

" But it is worst for poor Catharine, who was to have been a bride. See her sit like a stone in the sun! It is little any one can say to comfort Catharine."

The women, who knew no English, used soft Chippewa or Ottawa gutturals. The men who ventured on the conquerors' language used it shorn and contracted, as white children do.

The annual festivities of the Cross Village were at their height. Yells and the tumultuous patter of racing hoofs fell on Moses' ear. A trial of horse speed was now in progress; and later in the day would come a trial of agility and endurance in the Ottawa and Chippewa dances. The race-course was the mile-long street, beginning at the old chapel and ending at the monastery. Young Indians, vividly clad in red calico shirts and fringed leggings, leaned over their horses' necks, whipping and shouting. Dust rose behind the flying cavalcade, and spectators were obliged to keep close to the small carved houses or risk being run down. Young braves denied the war-path were obliged to give themselves unbridled range of some sort.

The monastery brethren had closed their whitewashed gates, not because they objected to the yearly fête, nor because custom made the monastery the goal in horse-racing, but because there was in the festivities an abandoned spirit to be dealt with only by the parish priest. On ordinary days the brethren were glad to show those beneficial death's heads with which their departed prior had ornamented the inner walls of his tomb before he came to use it. The village knew it had been that good prior's habit to sit in a coffin meditating, while he painted skulls and cross-bones in that roofed enclosure which was to be his body's last resting-place. Young squaws and braves often peeped at the completed grave and its surrounding symbols of mortality. It was as good as a Chippewa ghost-story.

The priest let himself be seen all the morning. Without speaking a word, he was a check upon the riotous. Ottawa and Chippewa had a right to commemorate some observances of their forefathers. He always winked at their dances. And this day the one silent Indian on the fence troubled him more than all the barbaric horsemen.

Moses' wife had been to him. Lucy was very indignant at her cousin Catharine. Moses neither ate nor slept, and he groaned in the night as if he had toothache. He would not talk to her. The good father might not believe it, but Catharine was putting a spell on Moses, in revenge for Frank Chibam. Catharine blamed Moses for everything —the shipwreck, the drowning, perhaps even for the storm. She hounded him out of the house and then she hounded him in again, by standing and looking at him with fixed gaze. It was more than flesh could bear. The father must see that Moses and Lucy would have to leave Cross Village and go to the Cheneaux or Mackinac, taking the grandmother with them. It would be hard for Moses to live without a boat. But then, Lucy demanded triumphantly, what would Catharine do without a man or any relation left in the house?

The priest looked from Catharine, motionless as a rock in the sun by the church gable, to Moses on the fence with his back towards her. The grandmother, oblivious to both, felt her way along the ground with a stick, and Lucy watched, nearer the grove. These four had occupied one of the small unpainted wooden houses as a united family. It was a sorrow to the priest that they might now be divided, one of them bearing an unconfessed trouble on his mind. For if Moses Nazagebic was as innocent as his wife Lucy believed him to be of the catastrophe which he said had happened on Lake Superior, he would not fly from poor Catharine as from an avenger.

There were fences of silver flattened out on the water; farther from shore flitted changeable bars of green and rose and pale-blue, converging until they swept the surface like some colossal peacock's tail. The grandmother stumping with her stick came quite near the cliff edge and stopped there. She was not blind or deaf, but her mind had long been turned inward and backward. She saw daily happenings as symbols of what had been.

She knew more tribal lore than any other Indian
of Cross Village ; and repeated, as she had repeated
a hundred times before when scanning the log dock
with its fleet of courtesying boats, the steep road,
and the strip of sand below :

"Down there was the first cross set up, many
years ago, by a man who came here in a large
boat moved by wings like the wings of a gull. The
man had a white face and long hair the color
of the sun. When he first landed he fell on his
knees and then began to count a string of beads.
Then he sang a song and called the other men,
some of whom were Indians, from the boat. They
cut down trees, and he made them set up a large
cross at the foot of the bluff. Since then that
strip of sand has been sacred, though the cross is
gone and a new one is set here by our priest."

The old squaw indicated with her stick the silver-
colored relic behind Moses Nazagebic. Her gut-
tural chant affected none of her hearers, except
that Catharine frowned at a sight which could
divert Moses. The Ottawas and Chippewas are a
hard-featured people. Catharine was, perhaps, the
handsomest product of an ill-favored village. Haggard pallor now encroached on the vermilion of her
cheek. She wore an old hat of plaited bark pulled
down to her eyes, and her strong black hair hung
in two neglected braids. The patience of aboriginal
womanhood was not stamped on her as it was on
Lucy. A panther could look no fiercer than this
lithe young Indian girl, whose bridal finery was

hid in the house and whose banns had been published in the mission church.

Trying to grapple with the trouble of Moses Nazagebic and Catharine, the priest also stood gazing at the dock, where children usually played, tumbling in to swim or be drawn out, only more roseate for the bath. The children were now gathered in the grove or along the race - course. Nothing moved below except lapping water. It was seldom that these lake - going people left their landing - place so deserted. Gliding down from the north where the cliff had screened it from view, came a small schooner. The priest, shaded by his broad hat, watched the passing craft with barely conscious recognition of it as an object until handkerchiefs fluttered from the deck and startled him.

The tall silver - white cross was so conspicuous that any one standing near it must be observed. The priest shook his handkerchief in reply. He had many friends along the coast and among the islands. But his long sight caught some familiar guise which made him directly signal and entreat with wide peremptory sweeps of the arm.

"Moses," commanded the priest, "you must unfasten a boat and go with me. There are people on board yonder that I want to see."

No other man being at hand, the request was a natural one, and Moses had been used to responding to such needs of the priest. But he cast a quick look at the black robe and sat sullenly until a stern repetition compelled him.

The priest had continued his signals, and the schooner came about and waited. It was not a long pull. Moses, rowing with his back towards the schooner, watched the face of his spiritual father.

"That will do," said the priest, and almost instantly some one on the schooner deck hailed him:

"Good-day, your reverence! What can we do for you?"

And another voice that Moses knew well shouted:

"Hello, Moses, is that you? Where's Frank? Did you get back all right with the sail-boat?"

The Indian cowered over his oars without answering or turning his head.

"I have come out," answered the priest, "to satisfy myself that I really see you here alive. We heard you were shipwrecked and drowned in Lake Superior."

"Shipwrecked, your reverence! What nonsense! We had a fine voyage and dismissed the men at the Sault. But since then we decided to make another cruise to the head of Lake Michigan, and hired another skipper. There is Moses in the boat with you, and Frank came home with him. They knew we were not shipwrecked."

"Will you land at Cross Village?"

"No, your reverence. We only tacked in to salute the cross in passing."

"But where shall I find you if I have urgent business with you?"

"At Little Traverse Bay. We cannot stop here."

The schooner was drifting away broadside, and the voice of the speaker came across a widening swell of water. Then she came up into her course, cutting a breastwork of foam in front of her as she passed on southward. With pantomime saluta- tions the priest and the two men who had hired Moses Nazagebic and Frank Chibain took leave of each other.

It had been a brief conference, but Moses rowed back a convicted criminal. He did not look at his conscience - keeper in the end of the boat. His high-cheeked face seemed to have had all individu- ality blotted out of it. Dazed and blear-eyed, he shipped his oars and tied the boat to its stake. A great noise of drumming and shouting came from the grove above, for the dances were soon to begin.

The steep road was a Calvary height to Moses. He dragged his feet as he climbed and stumbled in the deep sand; he who was so lithe of limb and nimble in any action. He had felt Catharine's eyes on his back like burning - glasses as he sat on the fence. They reflected on him now in one glare all the knowledge that the priest had gained of his crime. It was easier to follow to instant confession than to stay outside longer where Catharine could watch him. His wife's grandmother passed him, tapping along the fence and repeating again the legend of the first cross in Cross Village. Even in that day men who had slain their brothers were expected to give satisfaction to the tribe. It was either a life for a life or the labor of long hunting to solace a bereaved family.

He knelt down in the place where he had often confessed such little sins as lying or convivial drunkenness. How slight and innocent these offences seemed as the hopeless weight of this burden crushed him. The stern yet compassionate face over him exacted every word.

The priest remembered that this had not been a bad Chippewa. He had lived a steady, honest life in his humble station, keeping the three women well provided with such comforts as they needed; he had fished, he had labored at wood-chopping, and in the season helped Lucy fill her birch-bark mococks with maple sugar for sale at the larger settlements. The anguish of Cain was in the man's eyes. Natural life and he had already parted company. The teeth showed between his relaxed lips.

"Moses Nazagebic," said the priest, disregarding formula and dealing with the primitive sinner, "what have you done with Frank Chibam?"

"Father, I kill him."

The brief English which the Indian men mastered and used in their trading at the settlements was Moses' refuge in confession. To profane his native language with his crime seemed the last enormity of all.

"It was a lie that there was a wreck in Lake Superior?"

"Yes, father."

"It was a lie that you lost your sail-boat?"

"Yes, father."

"Did you intend to kill Frank?"

Moses swallowed as if his throat were closing.

"No—no! We both drunk. We quarrel; Frank sitting on edge of boat. I come up behind and hit him with oar. I knock him into the water."

"This was after the white men left you?"

"Yes, father. We have our money. We get drunk at Sault."

"Where is his body?"

"In St. Mary's River. Not far above Drummond Island."

"Are you sure he was drowned?"

"Oh, sure!" Moses' jaw dropped. "Frank he go down like a stone; and his spirit follow me ever since. His spirit tell Catharine. His spirit drive these men back so Cross Village know the truth. Good name, Chibam — that mean spirit. It follow me all the time. I get no rest till that spirit satisfied."

"My unhappy son, you must confess and give yourself up to justice."

"Justice no good. Justice hang. Frank Chibam want me go down like stone. Frank Chibam drive me back where he went down. But I not have my boat. Next thing Frank Chibam send me boat."

"What did you do with Frank's and yours?"

"I leave it at Drummond Island, with Chippewa there; and tell him to give it to nobody but Frank Chibam. I never set foot on that boat again—Frank's spirit angrier there than anywhere else."

"But how did you come home?"

"I get other Chippewa at Drummond to bring me to Mackinac. Then I get Chippewa at Mackinac to bring me to Cross Village. I tell last Chippewa I had a shipwreck. After Frank drowned I not know what to do. I had to come home. I thought if I said the boat was wrecked my people might believe me. I have to see Lucy." His bloodshot eyes piteously sought the compassion of his confessor. One moment's lapse into a brutal frenzy which now seemed some other man's had changed all things for him.

Never before had penitent come to that closet in such despair. Moses had repented through what seemed to him a long nightmare of succeeding days. There was no hope for him. He was called a Christian Indian, but the white man's consolations and ideas of retribution were not the red man's.

He heard the priest arrange a journey for him to give himself up to the law. The priest was a wise man, but this was uselessly clogging the wheels of fate. He did not want to sit in a jail with Frank Chibam's spirit. Such company was bad enough in the open sunlight. It was plain that neither Frank nor Catharine would be appeased by any offering short of their full measure of vengeance.

Having settled it that Moses' penance for his crime must be to give himself up to the law, the priest left him in the chapel and went out to press some sail-boat into service. It would be almost impossible to take any Indian from the festivities. The death of the most agile dancer and the withdrawal of the most ardent horse-racer had very mildly checked the usual joy.

Moses in his broken state was, perhaps, capable of sailing a boat, but it would be wiser to have another skipper aboard in crossing the strait to Mackinac.

It was fortunate, on the other hand, that the fête had prevented fishermen from hailing the passing schooner. The men were known by all the villagers, having stayed at the Cross Village inn, a place scarcely larger than a Chippewa cabin, kept by the only white family. These tribe remnants were gentle in their semi-civilization, yet the priest dreaded to think what might become of Moses if they discovered his lie and denied him the indulgence accorded to accidental man-killers.

To borrow a sail-boat would be easy enough while sympathy lasted for his penitent. He remembered also that Lucy could help sail it, and it would be best to take her to Mackinac for the parting with her husband.

The cross was stretching its afternoon shadow, and wind sweet with the moisture of many tossing blue miles flowed across the bluff. There never had been a fairer day for the yearly dances. Under his trouble the priest was conscious of trivial self-reproach that he had not told the passers it was fête day. But he reflected that few could love this remote little aboriginal world as he loved it, in joy or tragedy. The glamour of the North was over it through every season. At bleak January-end, in wastes of snow, the small houses were sealed and glowing with fires, and sledges creaked on the crust, while the shout of Indian children could be heard. Then the ice-boat shot out on the closed strait above and veered like a spirit from point to point, almost silent and terribly swift. On mornings after there had been a dry mist from the lake, this whole world was bridal-white, every twig loaded with frost blooms, until the far-reaching glory gave it a tropical beauty and lavishness and the frost fell like showers of flower petals.

His people stood respectfully out of his way as he entered the grove. The "throb, throb" and "pat, pat" of drum and feet were farther off, where young men were dancing in a ring. He could see their lithe bodies sway between tree boles. Old squaws sat with knees up to their chins, and old men smoked, pressing close to the spectacle. The priest was sensitive enough to feel a stir of uneasiness at his invasion of the aboriginal temple, and he was not long in having a boat put at his disposal.

The next thing was to induce Moses and Lucy to accompany him quietly down to the dock. He spoke to Lucy at her door. She sat in dull dejection, her basket-work and supply of sweet grass on the floor beside her.

"Come, Lucy! I have business in Mackinac, and Moses and you must take me there."

"Did that schooner bring you news, father?"

"Yes."

"But it is late."

"We may remain there to-night. Take such things with you as your husband might need for a week."

Lucy obediently put her basket-work away and prepared for the journey. She was conscious of triumph over Catharine, from whom the priest was about to rescue Moses. She put on her best sweet-grass hat and made up her bundle.

The priest brought Moses out of the chapel with a pity and tenderness that touched Lucy, and the three went down the steep road. Her grandmother was sitting in the sun by the gable and did not notice them. The old woman was telling herself the story of Nanabojou. The sail-boat which they were to take was anchored off the end of the dock. Moses rowed out after it and brought it alongside. He was busy raising the sails and the priest and Lucy had already taken their seats when the little craft answered to a light bound over the stern, and Catharine sat resolutely down, looking at Moses Nazagebic.

Moses let the sails fall and leaped out. He tied the rope to the dock.

"Get into the boat again, Moses!" commanded the priest. "And Catharine, you go back!"

Moses shook his head. His spirit was broken, but it was a physical impossibility for him to sail a boat to Mackinac with Catharine aboard.

The priest knew he might as well attempt to control gulls. French clamor or Anglo-Saxon brutality would be easy to persuade or compel, in comparison with this dense aboriginal silence. He took patience and sat still, reading his breviary. The boat ground softly against logs, and Lucy hugged her bundle, determined on the journey. Moses remained with his back to them, dangling his legs over the end of the dock. Catharine kept her place, grasping the edges of the craft. It was plain if Moses Nazagebic went to Mackinac it would be in the hands of officers sent to bring him at a later period. So the day dropped down in splendor, lake and sky becoming one dazzle of gold so bright the eye might not dwell on it. The party of four returned, and Catharine walked last up the hill. Religion and penance were nothing to a Chippewa girl who had distinct intentions of vengeance.

She kept an eye on her victim while she milked the cows as they came from the woods to keep their nightly appointment. The priest owned some lack in himself that he could not better handle the destinies around him. They hurt him, as rock would bruise tender flesh.

Barbaric instrumentation and shouting did not

keep him awake after darkness closed in. He would have lain awake if a dog had not stirred in Cross Village. He heard the wind change and strike the east side of his house with gusts of rain. Fires must die down to wet ashes in the grove. He knew the cross stood white and tall in scudding mist, and on the crosses in the cemetery chaplets and flowers made of white rags hung bedraggled. He foresaw the kind of day which would open before his poor penitent and be a symbol of the life that was to follow.

It was the priest himself who introduced Moses to this day, opening the door and standing unheeding under the overflow of the eaves. The hiss of rain could be heard, and daylight penetrated reluctantly abroad. Moses sat drooped forward with his elbows on his knees by the open fire. Lucy hurried to answer the summons, believing the priest had found some knew haven for Moses while her cousin was out of the house.

But there stood Catharine behind the priest, the spell of her fierceness broken, and at her side was Frank Chibam, undrowned and amiably grinning, his dark red skin stung by the weather, indeed, but otherwise little changed by water.

"Tell Moses I want him!" said the priest. "And Catharine, you go into the house!"

This time Catharine nimbly obeyed. As for Lucy, she made no outcry. She merely satisfied herself it was Frank Chibam before hurrying her husband to the spectacle.

Moses stepped out bareheaded into the rain, and his jaw dropped. The priest closed the door behind him.

Frank took his hand. Moses felt the young man's firm sinew and muscle. He looked piteously at the priest, his head sagging to one side, his face working in a spasm.

"I should have prepared him, Frank. This comes too suddenly on him."

They took Moses between them and walked with him along the fence at the foot of the cross. The raindrops moved down his face like tears. He did not speak, but listened with a child's intentness, first to one and then to the other, leaning his arm on his partner's shoulder.

"I don't understand why he was so certain he had killed you, Frank. He told me he struck you with an oar and saw you go down in the water like a stone."

"Whiskey, father," explained Frank in trader's brief English. "Plenty very bad whiskey. It make me sick for a week. The boom knocked us both down, and I fell into the water. The fisherman from one of the little islands who pull me out say that. Moses, he drunker than me; he too drunk to bring the boat home."

"The poor fellow told lies to cover the crime he thought he had committed. He has suffered, Frank. And I have suffered. We will say nothing about Catharine. Why didn't you come sooner?"

"I take the boat and go fishing. I say, 'Moses,

that lazy Chippewa, leave the boat for me to bring home; I make him wait for it.'"

"Did you quarrel at all?"

"Maybe so," said Frank. "Whiskey not let you remember much. But I could kill Moses easier than he could kill me."

"He has suffered enough. But you, my son, ought to do heavy penance."

"Not put off wedding?" suggested Frank, uneasily.

"I had not thought of unusual methods; it might be good discipline for Catharine, too. But we have lost enough cheer on your account."

"I never spend my money for whiskey any more, father. If some man ask me to take a drink, I drink with him, but not get drunk—no."

Moses laughed, his face shortening in horizontal lines.

"That Frank Chibam. Frank make me pay for all the whiskey. He not drowned. I not kill him. His spirit only an evil dream."

"The evil dream is now past, Moses," said the priest.

"Wake up, my brother!" said Frank in Chippewa. "I have a boatful of fish. You must come and help me with them. The good father will go back to his books when he sees you are yourself once more."

Under the rain-cloud the lake had turned to blue-black velvet water pricked with thousands of tossing white-caps. Near shore it seemed full of submerged smoke. And the rack tore itself, dragging low across the west. Moses, remembering the last sunset and its sickening splendors, felt that he had never seen so fine a day. He worked bareheaded and with his sleeves above his elbows among the fish. Gulls were flying, each making a burnished white glare against that background of weather. Looking up, the Chippewa could see the cross at the top of the bluff, standing over him in holy benediction. He felt lighter-bodied than a gull. And the anguish of that wretch who had sat on the fence believing himself a murderer was forgotten.

In the house his wife was exacting what in elder times would have been typified by an intricate piece of wampum, from her repentant cousin. Catharine brought in wood and carried water. Catharine was not permitted to make the great fish-pie, but could only look on. She served humbly. She had wronged her kinspeople by evil suspicion, and must make atonement. No words were lost between her and Lucy. She must lay her hand upon her mouth and be tasked until the elder woman was appeased. It was not the way of civilized women, but it was the aboriginal scheme, which the priest found good.

Lucy was not yet ready to demand the truth about the two white men and the shipwrecked boat. Her entire mind was given to humbling Catharine and impressing upon that forward young squaw that her husband was in no way accountable for the disappearance and vagrancy of Frank Chibam.

The grandmother basked at the hearth corner while this silent retribution went on unseen. She was repeating again the story of the first cross in Cross Village. She did not know that anything had happened in the house.

THE KING OF BEAVER

SUCCESS was the word most used by the King of Beaver. Though he stood before his people as a prophet assuming to speak revelations, executive power breathed from him. He was a tall, golden-tinted man with a head like a dome, hair curling over his ears, and soft beard and mustache which did not conceal a mouth cut thin and straight. He had student hands, long and well kept. It was not his dress, though that was careful as a girl's, which set him apart from farmers listening on the benches around him, but the keen light of his blue eyes, wherein shone the master.

Emeline thought she had never before seen such a man. He had an attraction which she felt loathsome, and the more so because it drew some part of her irresistibly to him. Her spirit was kin to his, and she resented that kinship, trying to lose herself among farmers' wives and daughters, who listened to their Prophet stolidly, and were in no danger of being naturally selected by him. This moral terror Emeline could not have expressed in words, and she hid it like a shame. She also resented the subservience of her kinspeople to one no greater than herself. Her stock had been masters of men.

As the King of Beaver slowly turned about the circle he encountered this rebel defying his assumption, and paused in his speaking a full minute, the drowsy farmers seeing merely that notes were being shifted and rearranged on the table. Then he began again, the dictatorial key transposed into melody. His covert message was to the new maid in the congregation. She might struggle like a fly in a web. He wrapped her around and around with beautiful sentences. As Speaker of the State Legislature he had learned well how to handle men in the mass, but nature had doubly endowed him for entrancing women. The spiritual part of James Strang, King and Prophet of a peculiar sect, appealed to the one best calculated to appreciate him during the remainder of his exhortation.

The Tabernacle, to which Beaver Island Mormons gathered every Saturday instead of every Sunday, was yet unfinished. Its circular shape and vaulted ceiling, panelled in the hard woods of the island, had been planned by the man who stood in the centre. Many openings under the eaves gaped windowless; but the congregation, sheltered from a July sun, enjoyed freely the lake air, bringing fragrance from their own fields and gardens. They seemed a bovine, honest people, in homespun and hickory; and youth, bright-eyed and fresh-cheeked, was not lacking. They sat on benches arranged in circles around a central platform which held the

Prophet's chair and table. This was his simple plan for making his world revolve around him.

Roxy Cheeseman, Emeline's cousin, was stirred to restlessness by the Prophet's unusual manner, and shifted uneasily on the bench. Her short, scarlet-cheeked face made her a favorite among the young men. She had besides this attraction a small waist and foot, and a father who was very well off indeed for a Beaver Island farmer. Roxy's black eyes, with the round and unwinking stare of a bird's, were fixed on King Strang, as if she instinctively warded off a gaze which by swerving a little could smite her.

But the Prophet paid no attention to any one when the meeting was over, his custom being to crush his notes in one hand at the end of his peroration, and to retire like a priest, leaving the dispersing congregation awed by his rapt face.

The two cousins walked sedately along the street of St. James village, while their elders lingered about the Tabernacle door shaking hands. That primitive settlement of the early '50's consisted of a few houses and log stores, a mill, the Tabernacle, and long docks, at which steamers touched perhaps once a week. The forest partially encircled it. A few Gentiles, making Saturday purchases in a shop kept by one of their own kind, glanced with dislike at the separating Mormons. The shouts of Gentile children could also be heard at Saturday play. Otherwise a Sabbath peacefulness was over the landscape. Beaver Island had not a rugged coastline, though the harbor of St. James was deep and good. Land rose from it in gentle undulations rather than hills.

Emeline and Roxy walked inland, with their backs to the harbor. In summer, farmers who lived nearest St. James took short-cuts through the woods to meeting, and let their horses rest.

The last house on the street was a wooden building of some pretension, having bow-windows and a veranda. High pickets enclosed a secluded garden. It was very unlike the log-cabins of the island.

" He lives here," said Roxy.

Emeline did not inquire who lived here. She understood, and her question was—

" How many with him ?"

" All of them—eight. Seven of them stay at home, but Mary French travels with him. Didn't you notice her in the Tabernacle—the girl with the rose in her hair, sitting near the platform ?"

" Yes, I noticed her. Was that one of his wives ?"

Roxy waited until they had struck into the woods path, and then looked guardedly behind her.

" Mary French is the youngest one. She was sealed to the Prophet only two years ago ; and last winter she went travelling with him, and we heard she dressed in men's clothes and acted as his secretary."

" But why did she do that when she was his wife according to your religion ?"

"I don't know," responded Roxy, mysteriously. "The Gentiles on the mainland are very hard on us."

They followed the track between fragrant grape-vine and hickory, and the girl bred to respect polygamy inquired—

"Do you feel afraid of the Prophet, Cousin Emeline?"

"No, I don't," retorted the girl bred to abhor it.

"Sometimes I do. He makes people do just what he wants them to. Mary French was a Gentile's daughter, the proudest girl that ever stepped in St. James. She didn't live on the island; she came here to visit. And he got her. What's the matter, Cousin Emeline?"

"Some one trod on my grave; I shivered. Cousin Roxy, I want to ask you a plain question. Do you like a man's having more than one wife?"

"No, I don't. And father doesn't either. But he was obliged to marry again, or get into trouble with the other elders. And Aunt Mahala is very good about the house, and minds mother. The revelation may be plain enough, but I am not the kind of a girl," declared Roxy, daringly, as one might blaspheme, "that cares a straw for the revelation."

Emeline took hold of her arm, and they walked on with a new sense of companionship.

"A great many of the people feel the same way about it. But when the Prophet makes them understand it is part of the faith, they have to keep the faith. I am a reprobate myself. But don't tell father," appealed Roxy, uneasily. "He is an elder."

"My uncle Cheeseman is a good man," said Emeline, finding comfort in this fact. She could not explain to her cousin how hard it had been for her to come to Beaver Island to live among Mormons. Her uncle had insisted on giving his orphan niece a home and the protection of a male relative, at the death of the maiden aunt by whom she had been brought up. In that day no girl thought of living without protection. Emeline had a few thousand dollars of her own, but her money was invested, and he could not count on the use of it, which men assumed a right to have when helpless women clustered to their hearths. Her uncle Cheeseman was undeniably a good man, whatever might be said of his religious faith.

"I like father myself," assented Roxy. "He is never strict with us unless the Prophet has some revelation that makes him so. Cousin Emeline, I hope you won't grow to be taken up with Brother Strang, like Mary French. I thought he looked at you to-day."

Emeline's face and neck were scarlet above her black dress. The Gentile resented as an insult what the Mormon simply foreboded as distasteful to herself; though there was not a family of that faith on the island who would not have felt honored in giving a daughter to the Prophet.

"I hate him!" exclaimed Emeline, her virgin rage

mingled with a kind of sweet and sickening pain. "I'll never go to his church again."

"Father wouldn't like that, Cousin Emeline," observed Roxy, though her heart leaped to such unshackled freedom. "He says we mustn't put our hand to the plough and turn back. Everybody knows that Brother Strang is the only person who can keep the Gentiles from driving us off the island. They have persecuted us ever since the settlement was made. But they are afraid of him. They cannot do anything with him. As long as he lives he is better than an army to keep our lands and homes for us."

"You are in a hard case betwixt Gentiles and Prophet," laughed Emeline.

Yet the aspects of life on Beaver Island keenly interested her. This small world, fifteen miles in length by six in breadth, was shut off by itself in Lake Michigan, remote from the civilization of towns. She liked at first to feel cut loose from her past life, and would have had the steamers touch less often at St. James, diminishing their chances of bringing her hateful news.

There were only two roads on the island — one extending from the harbor town in the north end to a village called Galilee at the extreme southeast end, the other to the southwest shore. Along these roads farms were laid out, each about eighty rods in width and a mile or two in length, so that neighbors dwelt within call of one another, and the colony presented a strong front. The King of Beaver

could scarcely have counselled a better division of
land for the linking of families. On one side of
the Cheesemans had dwelt an excellent widow with
a bag chin, and she became Elder Cheeseman's
second wife. On the other side were the Went-
worths, and Billy Wentworth courted Roxy across
the fence until it appeared that wives might con-
tinue passing over successive boundary lines.

The billowy land was green in the morning as
paradise, and Emeline thought every day its lights
and shadows were more beautiful than the day before. Life had paused in her, and she was glad to
rest her eyes on the horizon line and take no
thought about any morrow. She helped her cousin
and her legal and Mormon aunts with the children
and the cabin labor, trying to adapt herself to their
habits. But her heart-sickness and sense of fitting
in her place like a princess cast among peasants put
her at a disadvantage when, the third evening, the
King of Beaver came into the garden.

He chose that primrose time of day when the
world and the human spirit should be mellowest,
and walked with the farmer between garden beds
to where Emeline and Roxy were tending flowers.
The entire loamy place sent up incense. Emeline
had felt at least sheltered and negatively happy
until his voice modulations strangely pierced her,
and she looked up and saw him.

He called her uncle Brother Cheeseman and her
uncle called him Brother Strang, but on one side
was the mien of a sovereign and on the other the

deference of a subject. Again Emeline's blood rose against him, and she took as little notice as she dared of the introduction.

The King of Beaver talked to Roxy. Billy Wentworth came to the line fence and made a face at seeing him helping to tie up sweet-peas. Then Billy climbed over and joined Emeline. They exchanged looks, and each knew the mind of the other on the subject of the Prophet.

Billy was a good safe human creature, with the tang of the soil about him, and no wizard power of making his presence felt when one's back was turned. Emeline kept her gray eyes directed towards him, and talked about his day's work and the trouble of ploughing with oxen. She was delicately and sensitively made, with a beauty which came and went like flame. Her lips were formed in scarlet on a naturally pale face. Billy Wentworth considered her weakly. He preferred the robust arm outlined by Roxy's homespun sleeve. And yet she had a sympathetic knowledge of men which he felt, without being able to describe, as the most delicate flattery.

The King of Beaver approached Emeline. She knew she could not escape the interview, and continued tying vines to the cedar palisades while the two young islanders drew joyfully away to another part of the garden. The stable and barn-yard were between garden and cabin. Long variegated fields stretched off in bands. A gate let through the cedar pickets to a pasture where the cows came up to be milked. Bees gathering to their straw domes for the night made a purring hum at the other end of the garden.

"I trust you are here to stay," said Emeline's visitor.

"I am never going back to Detroit," she answered. He understood at once that she had met grief in Detroit, and that it might be other grief than the sort expressed by her black garment.

"We will be kind to you here."

Emeline, finishing her task, glanced over her shoulder at him. She did not know how tantalizingly her face, close and clear in skin texture as the petal of a lily, flashed out her dislike. A heavier woman's rudeness in her became audacious charm.

"I like Beaver Island," she remarked, winding the remaining bits of string into a ball. "'Every prospect pleases, and only man is vile.'"

"You mean Gentile man," said King Strang. "He is vile, but we hope to get rid of him some time."

"By breaking his fish-nets and stealing his sail-boats? Is it true that a Gentile sail-boat was sunk in Lake Galilee and kept hidden there until inquiry ceased, and then was raised, repainted, and launched again, a good Mormon boat?"

He linked his hands behind him and smiled at her daring.

"How many evil stories you have heard about us! My dear young lady, I could rejoin with truths about our persecutions. Is your uncle Cheeseman a malefactor?"

"My uncle Cheeseman is a good man."

"So are all my people. The island, like all young communities, is infested with a class of camp-followers, and every depredation of these fellows is charged to us. But we shall make it a garden—we shall make it a garden."

"Let me train vines over the whipping-post in your garden," suggested Emeline, turning back the crimson edge of her lip.

"You have heard that a man was publicly whipped on Beaver Island—and he deserved it. Have you heard also that I myself have been imprisoned by outsiders, and my life attempted more than once? Don't you know that in war a leader must be stern if he would save his people from destruction? Have you never heard a good thing of me, my child?"

Emeline, facing her adversary, was enraged at the conviction which the moderation and gentleness of a martyr was able to work in her.

"Oh yes, indeed, I have heard one good thing of you—your undertaking the salvation of eight or nine wives."

"Not yet nine," he responded, humorously. "And I am glad you mentioned that. It is one of our mysteries that you will learn later. You have helped me greatly by such a candid unburdening of your mind. For you must know that you and I are to be more to each other than strangers. The revelation was given to you when it was given to me in the Tabernacle. I saw that."

The air was thickening with dusky motes. Emeline fancied that living dark atoms were pressing down upon her from infinity.

"You must know," she said, with determination, "that I came to Beaver Island because I hated men, and expected to see nothing but Mormons here—"

"Not counting them men at all," indulgently supplemented the King of Beaver, conscious that she was struggling in the most masculine presence she had ever encountered. He dropped his voice. "My child, you touch me as no one has touched me yet. There is scarcely need of words between us. I know what I am to you. You shall not stay on the island if you do not wish it. Oh, you are going to make me do my best!"

"I wish you would go away!"

"Some Gentile has hurt you, and you are beating your bruised strength on me."

"Please go away! I don't like you. I am bound to another man."

"You are bound to nobody but me. I have waited a lifetime for you."

"How dare you talk so to me when you have eight wives already!"

"Solomon had a thousand. He was a man of God, though never in his life was there a moment when he took to his breast a mate. I shall fare better."

"Did you talk to them all like this?"

"Ask them. They have their little circles beyond which they cannot go. Have you thoughts in common with your cousin Roxy?"

"Yes, very many," asserted Emeline, doggedly. "I am just like Cousin Roxy."

"You have no mind beyond the milking and churning, the sewing and weaving?"

"No, I have no mind beyond them."

"I kiss your hands—these little hands that were made to the finest uses of life, and that I shall fill with honors."

"Don't touch me," warned Emeline. "They can scratch!"

The King of Beaver laughed aloud. With continued gentleness he explained to her: "You will come to me. Gentile brutes may chase women like savages, and maltreat them afterwards; but it is different with you and me." He brought his hands forward and folded them upright on his breast. "I have always prayed this prayer alone and as a solitary soul at twilight. For the first time I shall speak it aloud in the presence of one who has often thought the same prayer: O God, since Thou hast shut me up in this world, I will do the best I can, without fear or favor. When my task is done, let me out!"

He turned and left her, as if this had been a benediction on their meeting, and went from the garden as he usually went from the Tabernacle. Emeline's heart and eyes seemed to overflow without any volition of her own. It was a kind of spiritual effervescence which she could not control. She sobbed two or three times aloud, and immediately ground her teeth at his back as it passed out of sight. Billy and Roxy were so free from the baleful power that selected her. They could chat in peace under the growing darkness, they who had home and families, while she, without a relative except those on Beaver Island, or a friend whose duty it was to shelter her, must bear the shock of that ruinous force.

The instinct that no one could help her but herself kept her silent when she retired with Roxy to the loft-chamber. Primitive life on Beaver Island settled to its rest soon after the birds, and there was not a sound outside of nature's stirrings till morning, unless some drunken fishermen trailed down the Galilee road to see what might be inflicted on the property of sleeping Mormons.

The northern air blew fresh through gable windows of the attic, yet Emeline turned restlessly on her straw bed, and counted the dim rafters while Roxy slept. Finally she could not lie still, and slipped cautiously out of bed, feeling dire need to be abroad, running or riding with all her might. She leaned out of a gable window, courting the moist chill of the starless night. While the hidden landscape seemed strangely dear to her, she was full of unspeakable homesickness and longing for she knew not what—a life she had not known and could not imagine, some perfect friend who called her silently through space and was able to lift her out of the entanglements of existence.

The regular throbbing of a horse's feet approaching along the road at a brisk walk became quite

"I HAVE ALWAYS PRAYED THIS PRAYER ALONE"

AIMPHILIA

distinct. Emeline's sensations were suspended while she listened. From the direction of St. James she saw a figure on horseback coming between the dusky parallel fence rows. The sound of walking ceased in front of the house, and presently another sound crept barely as high as the attic window. It was the cry of a violin, sweet and piercing, like some celestial voice. It took her unawares. She fled from it to her place beside Roxy and covered her ears with the bedclothes.

Roxy turned with a yawn and aroused from sleep. She rose to her elbow and drew in her breath, giggling. The violin courted like an angel, finding secret approaches to the girl who lay rigid with her ears stopped.

"Cousin Emeline!" whispered Roxy, "do you hear that?"

"What is it?" inquired Emeline, revealing no emotion.

"It's Brother Strang serenading."

"How do you know?"

"Because he is the only man on Beaver who can play the fiddle like that." Roxy gave herself over to unrestrained giggling. "A man fifty years old!"

"I don't believe it," responded Emeline, sharply.

"Don't believe he is nearly fifty? He told his age to the elders."

"I haven't a word of praise for him, but he isn't an old man. He doesn't look more than thirty-five."

"To hear that fiddle you'd think he wasn't

twenty," chuckled Roxy. "It's the first time Brother Strang ever came serenading down this road."

He did not stay long, but went, trailing music deliciously into the distance. Emeline knew how he rode, with the bridle looped over his bow arm. She was quieted and lay in peace, sinking to sleep almost before the faint, far notes could no longer be heard.

From that night her uncle Cheeseman's family changed their attitude towards her. She felt it as a withdrawal of intimacy, though it expressed reverential awe. Especially did her Mormon aunt Mahala take little tasks out of her hands and wait upon her, while her legal aunt looked at her curiously. It was natural for Roxy to talk to Billy Wentworth across the fence, but it was not natural for them to share so much furtive laughter, which ceased when Emeline approached. Uncle Cheeseman himself paid more attention to his niece and spent much time at the table explaining to her the Mormon situation on Beaver Island, tracing the colony back to its secession from Brigham Young's party in Illinois.

"Brother Strang was too large for them," said her uncle. "He can do anything he undertakes to do."

The next Saturday Emeline refused to go to the Tabernacle. She gave no reason and the family asked for none. Her caprices were as the gambols of the paschal lamb, to be indulged and overlooked. Roxy offered to stay with her, but she rejected

"IT'S BROTHER STRANG SERENADING"

companionship, promising her uncle and aunts to lock herself within the cabin and hide if she saw men approaching from any direction. The day was sultry for that climate, and of a vivid clearness, and the sky dazzled. Emeline had never met any terrifying Gentiles during her stay on the island, and she felt quite secure in crossing the pasture and taking to the farm woods beyond. Her uncle's cows had worn a path which descended to a run with partially grass-lined channel. Beaver Island was full of brooks and springs. The children had placed stepping-stones across this one. She was vaguely happy, seeing the water swirl below her feet, hearing the cattle breathe at their grazing; though in the path or on the log which she found at the edge of the woods her face kept turning towards the town of St. James, as the faces of the faithful turn towards Mecca. It was childish to think of escaping the King of Beaver by merely staying away from his exhortations. Emeline knew she was only parleying.

The green silence should have helped her to think, but she found herself waiting—and doing nothing but waiting—for what might happen next. She likened herself to a hunted rabbit palpitating in cover, unable to reach any place of safety yet grateful for a moment's breathing. Wheels rolled southward along the Galilee road. Meeting was out. She had the caprice to remain where she was when the family wagon arrived, for it had been too warm to walk to the Tabernacle. Roxy's voice called her, and as she answered, Roxy skipped across the brook and ran to her.

"Cousin Emeline," the breathless girl announced, "here comes Mary French to see you!"

Emeline stiffened upon the log.

"Where?"

Roxy glanced behind at a figure following her across the meadow.

"What does she want of me?" inquired Emeline. "If she came home with the family, it was not necessary to call me."

"She drove by herself. She says Brother Strang sent her to you."

Emeline stood up as the Prophet's youngest wife entered that leafy silence. Roxy, forgetting that these two had never met before, slipped away and left them. They looked at each other.

"How do you do, Mrs. Strang?" spoke Emeline.

"How do you do, Miss Cheeseman?" spoke Mary French.

"Will you sit down on this log?"

"Thank you."

Mary French had more flesh and blood than Emeline. She was larger and of a warmer and browner tint—that type of brunette with startling black hair which breaks into a floss of little curls, and with unexpected blue eyes. Her full lips made a bud, and it only half bloomed when she smiled. From crown to slipper she was a ripe and supple woman. Though clad, like Emeline, in black, her garment was a transparent texture over white, and she held a parasol with crimson lining behind her head. She had left her bonnet in her conveyance.

"My husband," said Mary French, quiet and smiling, "sent me to tell you that you will be welcomed into our family."

Emeline looked her in the eyes. The Prophet's wife had the most unblenching smiling gaze she had ever encountered.

"I do not wish to enter your family. I am not a Mormon."

"He will make you wish it. I was not a Mormon."

They sat silent, the trees stirring around them.

"I do not understand it," said Emeline. "How can you come to me with such a message?"

"I can do it as you can do it when your turn comes."

Emeline looked at Mary French as if she had been stabbed.

"It hurts, doesn't it?" said Mary French. "But wait till he seems to you a great strong archangel —an archangel with only the weakness of dabbling his wings in the dirt—and you will withhold from him nothing, no one, that may be of use to him. If he wants to put me by for a while, it is his will. You cannot take my place. I cannot fill yours."

"Oh, don't!" gasped Emeline. "I am not that sort of woman—I should kill!"

"That is because you have not lived with him. I would rather have him make me suffer than not have him at all."

"Oh, don't! I can't bear it! Help me!" prayed Emeline, stretching her hands to the wife.

Mary French met her with one hand and the unflinching smile. Her flesh was firm and warm, while Emeline's was cold and quivering.

"You have never loved anybody, have you?"

"No."

"But you have thought you did?"

"I was engaged before I came here."

"And the engagement is broken?"

"We quarrelled."

Mary French breathed deeply.

"You will forget it here. He can draw the very soul out of your body."

"He cannot!" flashed Emeline.

"Some one will kill him yet. He is not understood at his best, and he cannot endure defeat of any kind. When you come into the family you must guard him from his enemies as I have constantly guarded him. If you ever let a hair of his head be harmed—then I shall hate you!"

"Mrs. Strang, do you come here to push me too? My uncle's family, everything, all are closing around me! Why don't you help me? I loathe—I loathe your husband!"

Mary French rose, her smile changing only to express deep tenderness.

"You are a good girl, dear. I can myself feel your charm. I was not so self-denying. In my fierce young girlhood I would have removed a rival. But since you ask me, I will do all I can for you in the way you desire. My errand is done. Good-by."

"Good-by," said Emeline, restraining herself.

She sat watching the elastic shape under the parasol move with its shadow across the field. She had not a doubt until Mary French was gone; then the deep skill of the Prophet's wife with rivals sprung out like a distortion of nature.

Emeline had nearly three weeks in which to intrench herself with doubts and defences. She felt at first surprised and relieved. When her second absence from the Tabernacle was passed over in silence she found in her nature an unaccountable pique, which steadly grew to unrest. She ventured and turned back on the woods path leading to St. James many times, each time daring farther. The impulse to go to St. James came on her at waking, and she resisted through busy hours of the day. But the family often had tasks from which Emeline was free, and when the desire grew unendurable she knelt at her secluded bedside in the loft, trying to bring order out of her confused thoughts. She reviewed her quarrel with her lover, and took blame for his desertion. The grievance which had seemed so great to her before she came to Beaver Island dwindled, and his personality with it. In self-defence she coaxed her fancy, pretending that James Arnold was too good for her. It was well he had found it out. But because he was too good for her she ought to go on being fond of him at a safe distance, undetected by him, and discreetly cherish-

ing his large blond image as her ideal of manhood.
If she had not been bred in horror of Catholics, the
cloister at this time would have occurred to her as
her only safe refuge.

These secret rites in her bedroom being ended,
and Roxy diverted from her movements, she slipped
off into the woods path, sometimes running breath-
lessly towards St. James.

The impetus which carried Emeline increased
with each journey. At first she was able to check
it in the woods depths, but it finally drove her until
the village houses were in sight.

When this at last happened, and she stood gazing,
fascinated, down the tunnel of forest path, the
King of Beaver spoke behind her.

Emeline screamed in terror and took hold of a bush,
to make it a support and a veil.

"Have I been a patient man?" he inquired, standing between her and her uncle's house. "I waited
for you to come to me."

"I am obliged to go somewhere," said Emeline,
plucking the leaves and unsteadily shifting her eyes
about his feet. "I cannot stay on the farm all the
time." Through numbness she felt the pricking of
a sharp rapture.

The King of Beaver smiled, seeing betrayed in
her face the very vertigo of joy.

"You will give yourself to me now?" he winning-
ly begged, venturing out-stretched hands. "You
have felt the need as I have? Do you think the
days have been easy to me? When you were on

"'YOU WILL GIVE YOURSELF TO ME NOW?'"

your knees I was on my knees too. Every day you came in this direction I came as far as I dared, to meet you. Are the obstacles all passed?"

"No," said Emeline.

He was making her ask herself that most insidious question, "Why could not the other have been like this?"

"Tell me—can you say, 'I hate you,' now?"

"No," said Emeline.

"I have grown to be a better man since you said you hated me. The miracle cannot be forced. Next time?" He spoke wistfully.

"No," Emeline answered, holding to the bush. She kept her eyes on the ground while he talked, and glanced up when she replied. He stood with his hat off. The flakes of sun touched his head and the fair skin of his forehead.

He moved towards Emeline, and she retreated around the bush. Without hesitating he passed, making a salutation, and went on by himself to St. James. She watched his rapid military walk furtively, her eyebrows crouching, her lips rippling with passionate tremors. Then she took to flight homeward, her skirts swishing through the woods with a rush like the wind. The rebound was as violent as the tension had been.

There were few festivities on Beaver Island, the Mormon families living a pastoral life, many of them yet taxed by the struggle for existence. Crops shot up rank and strong in the short Northern summer. Soft cloud masses sailed over the island,

and rain-storms marched across it with drums of thunder which sent reverberations along the water world. Or fogs rolled in, muffling and obliterating homesteads.

Emeline stayed in the house, busying herself with the monotonous duties of the family three days. She was determined never to go into the woods path again without Roxy. The fourth day a gray fog gave her no choice but imprisonment. It had the acrid tang of smoke from fires burning on the mainland. About nightfall the west wind rose and blew it back, revealing a land mantled with condensed drops.

Emeline put on her hat and shawl to walk around in the twilight. The other young creatures of the house were glad to be out also, and Roxy and Roxy's lover talked across the fence. Emeline felt fortified against the path through the woods at night; yet her feet turned in that direction, and as certainly as water seeks its level she found herself on the moist elastic track. Cow-bells on the farm sounded fainter and farther. A gloom of trees massed around her, and the forest gave up all its perfume to the dampness.

At every step she meant to turn back, though a recklessness of night and of meeting the King of Beaver grew upon her. Thus, without any reasonable excuse for her presence there, she met Mary French.

" Is that you, Miss Cheeseman?" panted the Prophet's youngest wife.

Emeline confessed her identity.

"I was coming for you, but it is fortunate you are so far on the way. There is a steamboat at the dock, and it will go out in half an hour. I could not get away sooner to tell you." Mary French breathed heavily from running. "When the steamboat came in the captain sent for my husband, as the captains always do. I went with him: he knows how I dread to have him go alone upon a boat since an attempt was made last year to kidnap him. But this time there was another reason, for I have been watching. And sure enough, a young man was on the steamboat inquiring where he could find you. His name is James Arnold. The captain asked my husband to direct him to you. You will readily understand why he did not find you. Come at once!"

"I will not," said Emeline.

"But you wanted me to help you, and I have been trying to do it. We easily learned by letter from our friends in Detroit who your lover was. My husband had me do that: he wanted to know. Then without his knowledge I stooped to write an anonymous letter."

"To James Arnold?"

"Yes."

"About me?"

"About you."

"What did you tell him?"

"I said you were exposed to great danger on Beaver Island, among the Mormons, and if you had

any interested friend it was time for him to inter-
fere."

"And that brought him here?"

"I am sure it did. He was keenly disappointed
at not finding you."

"But why didn't he come to the farm?"

"My husband prevented that. He said you were
on Beaver Island three or four weeks ago, but you
were now in the Fairy Isle. It was no lie. He
spoke in parables, but the other heard him literally.
We let him inquire of people in St. James. But
no one had seen you since the Saturday you came
to the Tabernacle. So he is going back to Mackinac
to seek you. Your life will be decided in a quarter
of an hour. Will you go on that steamboat?"

"Throw myself on the mercy of a man who dared
—*dared* to break his engagement, and who ought
to be punished and put on probation, and then refused! No, I cannot!"

"The minutes are slipping away."

"Besides, I have nothing with me but the clothes
I have on. And my uncle's family—think of my
uncle's family!"

"You can write to your uncle and have him send
your baggage. I dare not carry any messages.
But I thought of what you would need to-night,
and put some things and some money in this satchel.
They were mine. Keep them all."

Emeline took hold of the bag which Mary French
shoved in her hand. Their faces were indistinct to
each other.

"'LET ME LOOSE!' STRUGGLED EMELINE"

"For the first time in my life I have deceived my husband!"

"Oh, what shall I do—what shall I do?" cried the girl.

A steamer whistle at St. James dock sent its bellow rebounding from tree to tree in the woods. Emeline seized Mary French and kissed her violently on both cheeks. She snatched the bag and flew towards St. James.

"Stop!" commanded the Prophet's wife.

She ran in pursuit, catching Emeline by the shoulders.

"You sha'n't go! What am I doing? Maybe robbing him of what is necessary to his highest success! I am a fool—to think he might turn back to me for consolation when you are gone—God forgive me such silly fondness! I can't have a secret between him and myself—I will tell him! You shall not go—and cause him a mortal hurt! Wait! —stop!—the boat is gone! It's too late!"

"Let me loose!" struggled Emeline, wrenching herself away.

She ran on through the woods, and Mary French, snatching at garments which eluded her, stumbled and fell on the damp path, gathering dead leaves under her palms. The steamer's prolonged bellow covered her voice.

Candles were lighted in St. James. The Tabernacle spread itself like a great circular web dark with moisture. Emeline was conscious of running across the gang-plank as a sailor stooped to draw it in. The bell was ringing and the boat was already in motion. It sidled and backed away from its moorings.

Emeline knelt panting at the rail on the forward deck. A flambeau fastened to the wharf bowed its light to the wind as the boat swung about, showing the King of Beaver smiling and waving his hand in farewell. He did not see Emeline. His farewell was for the man whom he had sent away without her. His golden hair and beard and blue eyes floated into Emeline's past as the steamer receded, the powerful face and lithe figure first losing their identity, and then merging into night. What if it was true that she was robbing both him and herself of the best life, as Mary French was smitten to believe at the last moment? Her Gentile gorge rose against him, and the traditions of a thousand years warred in her with nature; yet she stretched her hands towards him in the darkness.

Then she heard a familiar voice, and knew that the old order of things was returning, while Beaver Island, like a dream, went silently down upon the waters.

Some years later, in the '50's, Emeline, sitting opposite her husband at the breakfast-table, heard him announce from the morning paper:

"Murder of King Strang, the Mormon Prophet of Beaver Island." All the details of the affair, even the track of the bullets which crashed into that golden head, were mercilessly printed. The reader, surprised by a sob, dropped his paper.

"What! Are you crying, Mrs. Arnold?"

"It was so cruel!" sobbed Emeline. "And Billy Wentworth, like a savage, helped to do it!"

"He had provocation, no doubt, though it is a horrid deed. Perhaps I owe the King of Beaver the tribute of a tear. He befogged me considerably the only time I ever met him."

"You see only his evil. But I see what he was to Mary French and the others."

"His bereaved widows?"

"The ones who believed in his best."

BEAVER LIGHTS

A MAGNIFICENT fountain of flame, visible far out on the starlit lake, spurted from the north end of Beaver Island. It was the temple, in which the Mormon people had worshipped for the last time, sending sparks and illumined vapor to the zenith. The village of St. James was partly in ashes, and a blue pallor of smoke hung dimly over nearly every hill and hollow, for Gentile fishermen crazed with drink and power and long arrears of grievances had carried torch and axe from farm to farm. Until noon of that day all householding families had been driven to huddle with their cattle around the harbor dock and forced to make pens for the cattle of lumber which had been piled there for transportation. Unresisting as sheep they let themselves be shipped on four small armed steamers sent by their enemies to carry them into exile. Not one of the twelve elders who had received the last instructions of their murdered king rose up to organize any defence. Scarcely a month had passed since his wounding unto death, and his withdrawal, like Arthur, in the arms of weeping women to that spot in Wisconsin where he had found his sacred Voree plates or tables of the law. Scarcely two weeks had passed since news came back of his burial there. And already the Mormon settlement was swept off Beaver Island.

Used to border warfare and to following their dominating prophet to victory, they yet seemed unable to strike a blow without him. Such non-resistance procured them nothing but contempt. They even submitted to being compelled to destroy a cairn raised over the grave of one considered a malefactor, carrying the heap stone by stone to throw into the lake, Gentiles standing over them like Egyptian masters.

Little waves ran in rows of light, washing against the point on the north side of the landlocked harbor. A primrose star was there struggling aloft at the top of a rough rock tower. It was the fish-oil flame of Beaver lamp, and the keeper sat on his doorsill at the bottom of the light-house with his wife beside him.

The lowing of cattle missing their usual evening tendance came across from the dock, a mournful accompaniment to the distant roaring of fire and falling of timbers.

"Do you realize, Ludlow," the young woman inquired, slipping her hand into her husband's, "that I am now the only Mormon on Beaver Island?"

"You never were a very good Mormon, Cecilia. You didn't like the breed any better than I did, though there were good people among them."

"Will they lose all their cattle, Ludlow?"

119

"The cattle are safe enough," he laughed. "The men that are doing this transporting will take the cattle. None of our Mormon friends will ever see a hoof from Beaver Island again."

"But it seems robbery to drive them off and seize their property."

"That's the way King Strang took Beaver from the Gentiles in the first place. Mormons and Gentiles can't live together."

"We can."

"I told you that you were a poor Mormon, Cecilia. And from first to last I opposed my family's entering the community. Tithes and meddling sent my father out of it a poor man. But I'm glad he went before this; and your people, too."

She drew a deep breath. "Oh yes! They're safe in Green Bay. I couldn't endure to have them on those steamers going down the lake to-night. What will become of the community, Ludlow?"

"God knows. They'll be landed at Chicago and turned adrift on the world. I'm glad they're away from here. I've no cause to love them, but I was afraid they would be butchered like sheep. Your father and my father, if they had still been elders on the island, wouldn't have submitted, as these folks did, to abuse and exile and the loss of everything they had in the world. I can't understand it of some of them. There was Jim Baker, for instance; I'd have sworn he would fight."

"I can understand why he didn't. He hasn't taken any interest since his second marriage."

"Now, that was a nice piece of work! I always liked Jim the best of any of the young men until he did that. And what inducement was there in the woman?"

The light-house keeper's wife fired up. "What inducement there was for him ever to marry Rosanne I couldn't see. And I know Elizabeth Aiken loved him when we were girls together."

"And didn't Rosanne?"

"Oh—Rosanne! A roly-poly spoiled young one, that never will be a woman! Elizabeth is noble."

"You're fond of Elizabeth because she was witness to our secret marriage when King Strang wouldn't let me have you. I liked Jim for the same reason. Do you mind how we four slipped one at a time up the back stairs in my father's house that night, while the young folks were dancing below?"

"I mind we picked Elizabeth because Rosanne would be sure to blab, even if she had to suffer herself for it. How scared the poor elder was!"

"We did him a good turn when we got him to marry us. He'd be on one of the steamers bound for nowhere, to-night, instead of snug at Green Bay, if we hadn't started him on the road to what King Strang called disaffection."

The light-house keeper jumped up and ran out on the point, his wife following him in nervous dread.

"What is the matter, Ludlow?"

Their feet crunched gravel and paused where ripples still ran in, endlessly bringing lines of dimmer and dimmer light. A rocking boat was tied to a stake. Anchored and bare-masted, farther out in the mouth of the bay, a fishing-smack tilted slightly in rhythmic motion. While they stood a touch of crimson replaced the sky light in the water, and great blots like blood soaking into the bay were reflected from the fire. The burning temple now seemed to rise a lofty tower of flame against the horizon. Figures could be seen passing back and forth in front of it, and shouts of fishermen came down the peninsula. The King's printing-office where the *Northern Islander* was once issued as a daily had smouldered down out of the way. It was the first place to which they had set torch.

"I thought I heard some one running up the sail on our sail-boat," said the light-house keeper. "No telling what these fellows may do. If they go to meddling with me in my little Government office, they'll find me as stubborn as the Mormons did."

"Oh, Ludlow, look at the tabernacle, like a big red-hot cheese-box on the high ground! Think of the coronation there on the first King's Day!"

The light-house keeper's wife was again in imagination a long-limbed girl of fifteen, crowding into the temple to witness such a ceremony as was celebrated on no other spot of the New World. The King of Beaver, in a crimson robe, walked the temple aisle, followed by his council, his twelve elders, and seventy ministers of the minor order. In the presence of a hushed multitude he was anointed, and a crown with a cluster of projecting stars was set on his golden head. Hails and shouts, music of marching singers and the strewing of flowers went before him into the leafy July woods. Thus King's Day was established and annually observed on the 8th of July. It began with burnt-offerings. The head of each family was required to bring a chicken. A heifer was killed and carefully cut up without breaking a bone; and, while the smoke of sacrifice arose, feasting and dancing began, and lasted until sunset. Firstlings of flocks and the first-fruits of orchard and field were ordained the King's; and he also claimed one-tenth of each man's possessions. The Mosaic law was set up in Beaver Island, even to the stoning of rebellious children.

The smoke of a sacrificed people was now reeking on Beaver. This singular man's French ancestry —for he was descended from Henri de L'Estrange, who came to the New World with the Duke of York—doubtless gave him the passion for picturesqueness and the spiritual grasp on his isolated kingdom which keeps him still a notable and unforgotten figure.

"It makes me feel bad to see so much destruction," the young man said to his wife; "though I offered to go with Billy Wentworth to shoot Strang if nobody else was willing. I knew I was marked, and sooner or later I would disappear if he continued to govern this island. But with all his faults he was a man. He could fight; and whip. He'd have sunk every steamer in the harbor to-day."

"It's heavy on my heart, Ludlow—it's dreadful! Neighbors and friends that we shall never see again!"

The young man caught his wife by the arm. They both heard the swift beat of footsteps flying down the peninsula. Cecilia drew in her breath and crowded against her husband. A figure came into view and identified itself, leaping in bisected draperies across an open space to the light-house door.

"Why, Rosanne!" exclaimed the keeper's wife. She continued to say "Why, Rosanne! Why, Rosanne Baker!" after she had herself run into the house and lighted a candle.

She set the candle on the chimney. It showed her rock-built domicile, plain but dignified, like the hollow of a cavern, with blue china on the cupboard shelves and a spinning-wheel standing by the north wall. A corner staircase led to the second story of the tower, and on its lowest step the fugitive dropped down, weeping and panting. She was peculiarly dressed in the calico bloomers which the King of Beaver had latterly decreed for the women of his kingdom. Her trim legs and little feet, cased in strong shoes, appeared below the baggy trousers. The upper part of her person, her almond eyes, round curves and features were full of Oriental suggestions. Some sweet inmate of a harem might so have materialized, bruising her softness against the hard stair.

"Why, Rosanne Baker!" her hostess reiterated.

Cecilia did not wear bloomers. She stood erect in petticoats. "I thought you went on one of the boats!"

"I didn't," sobbed Rosanne. "When they were crowding us on I slipped among the lumber piles and hid. I've been hid all day, lying flat between boards — on top where they couldn't see me."

"Suppose the lumber had been set on fire, too! And you haven't had anything to eat?"

"I don't want to eat. I'm only frightened to death at the wicked Gentiles burning the island. I couldn't stay there all night, so I got down and ran to your house."

"Of course, you poor child! But, Rosanne, where's your husband?"

The trembling creature stiffened herself and looked at Cecilia out of the corners of her long eyes. "He's with Elizabeth Aiken."

The only wife of one husband did not know how to take hold of this subject.

"But your father was there," she suggested. "How could you leave your father and run the risk of never seeing him again?"

"I don't care if I never see him again. He said he was so discouraged he didn't care what became of any of us."

Cecilia was going to plead the cause of domestic affection further, but she saw that four step-mothers could easily be given up. She turned helplessly to her husband who stood in the door.

"Poor thing! Ludlow, what in the world shall we do?"

"Put her to bed."

"Of course, Ludlow. But will anybody hurt you to-morrow?"

"There are two good guns on the rack over the chimney. I don't think anybody will hurt me or her either, to-morrow."

"Rosanne, my dear," said Cecilia, trying to lift the relaxed soft body and to open the stairway door behind her. "Come up with me right off. I think you better be where people cannot look in at us."

Rosanne yielded and stumbled to her feet, clinging to her friend. When they disappeared the young man heard her through the stairway enclosure sobbing with convulsive gasps:

"I hate Elizabeth Aiken! I wish they would kill Elizabeth Aiken! I hate her—I hate her!"

The lighthouse-keeper sat down again on his doorstep and faced the prospect of taking care of a homeless Mormon. It appeared to him that his wife had not warmly enough welcomed her or met the situation with that recklessness one needed on Beaver Island. The tabernacle began to burn lower, brands streaming away in the current which a fire makes. It was strange to be more conscious of inland doings than of that vast unsalted sea so near him, which moistened his hair with vaporous drifts through the darkness. The garnet redness of the temple shed a huger amphitheatre of shine around itself. A taste of acrid smoke was on his lips. He was considering that drunken fishermen might presently begin to rove, and he would be wiser to go in and shut the house and put out his candle, when by stealthy approaches around the lighthouse two persons stood before him.

"Is Ludlow here?" inquired a voice which he knew.

"I'm here, Jim! Are all the Mormons coming back?"

"Is Rosanne in your house?"

"Rosanne is here; up-stairs with Cecilia. Come inside, Jim. Have you Elizabeth with you?"

"Yes, I have Elizabeth with me."

The three entered together. Ludlow shut the door and dropped an iron bar across it. The young men standing opposite were of nearly the same age; but one was fearless and free and the other harassed and haggard. Out-door labor and the skill of the fisheries had given to both depth of chest and clean, muscular limbs. But James Baker had the desperate and hunted look of a fugitive from justice. He was fair, of the strong-featured, blue-eyed type that has pale chestnut-colored hair clinging close to a well-domed head.

"Yes, Rosanne is here," Ludlow repeated. "Now will you tell me how you got here?"

"I rowed back in a boat."

"Who let you have a boat?"

"There were sailors on the steamer. After I found Rosanne was left behind I would have had a boat or killed the man that prevented me. I had to wait out on the lake until it got dark. I knew your wife would take care of her. I told myself that when I couldn't find any chance to land in St. James's Bay until sunset."

"She's been hiding in the lumber on the dock all day."

"Did any one hurt her?"

"Evidently not."

The Mormon husband's face cleared with a convulsion which in woman would have been a relieving burst of tears.

"Sit down, Elizabeth," said the lighthouse-keeper. "You look fit to fall."

"Yes, sit down, Elizabeth," James Baker repeated, turning to her with secondary interest. But she remained standing, a tall Greek figure in bloomers, so sure of pose that drapery or its lack was an accident of which the eye took no account. She had pushed her soft brown hair, dampened by the lake, behind her ears. They showed delicately against the two shining masses. Her forehead and chin were of noble and courageous shape. If there was fault, it was in the breadth and height of brows masterful rather than feminine. She had not one delicious sensuous charm to lure man. Her large eyes were blotted with a hopeless blankness. She waited to see what would be done next.

"Now I'll tell you," said Baker to his friend, with decision, "I'm not going to bring the howling Gentiles around you."

"I don't care whether they come or not."

"I know you don't. It isn't necessary in such a time as this for you and me to look back."

"I told you at the time I wouldn't forget it, Jim. You stood by me when I married Cecilia in the teeth of the Mormons, and I'll stand by you through any mob of Gentiles. My sail-boat's out yonder, and it's yours as long as you want it; and we'll provision it."

"That's what I was going to ask, Ludlow."

"If I were you I'd put for Green Bay. Old neighbors are there, my father among them."

"That was my plan!"

"But," Ludlow added, turning his thumb over his shoulder with embarrassment, "they're all Gentiles in Green Bay."

"Elizabeth and I talked it over in the boat. I told her the truth before God. We've agreed to live apart. Ludlow, I never wanted any wife but Rosanne, and I don't want any wife but Rosanne now. You don't know how it happened; I was first of the young men called on to set an example. Brother Strang could bring a pressure to bear that it was impossible to resist. He might have threatened till doomsday. But I don't know what he did with me. I told him it wasn't treating Elizabeth fair. Still, I married her according to Saints' law, and I consider myself bound by my pledge to provide for her. She's a good girl. She has no one to look to but me. And I'm not going to turn her off to shift for herself if the whole United States musters against me."

"Now you talk like a man. I think better of you than I have for a couple of weeks past."

"It ought to make me mad to be run off of Beaver. But I couldn't take any interest. May I see Rosanne?"

"Go right up-stairs. Cecilia took her up to put her to bed. The walls and floors are thick here or she would have heard your voice."

"Poor little Rosanne! It's been a hard day for her."

The young Mormon paused before ascending. "Ludlow, as soon as you can give me a few things to make the women comfortable for the run to Green Bay, I'll take them and put out."

"Tell Cecilia to come down. She'll know what they need."

Until Cecilia came down and hugged Elizabeth silently but most tenderly the lighthouse-keeper stood with his feet and gaze planted on a braided rug, not knowing what to say. He then shifted his feet and remarked:

"It's a fine night for a sail, Elizabeth. I think we're going to have fair weather."

"I think we are," she answered.

Hurried preparations were made for the voyage. Elizabeth helped Cecilia gather food and clothes and two Mackinac blankets from the stores of a young couple not rich but open-handed. The light-house-keeper trimmed the lantern to hang at the mast-head. He was about to call the two up-stairs when the crunching of many feet on gravel was heard around his tower and a torch was thrust at one of the windows.

At the same instant he put Elizabeth and Cecilia in the stairway and let James Baker, bounding down three steps at once, into the room.

Each man took a gun, Ludlow blowing out the candle as he reached for his weapons.

"Now you stand back out of sight and let me talk to them," he said to the young Mormon, as an explosive clamor began. "They'll kill you, and they daren't touch me. Even if they had anything against me, the drunkest of them know better than to shoot down a government officer. I'm going to open this window."

A rabble of dusky shapes headed by a torch-bearer who had doubtless lighted his fat-stick at the burning temple, pressed forward to force a way through the window.

"Get off of the flower-bed," said Ludlow, dropping the muzzle of his gun on the sill. " You're tramping down my wife's flowers."

"It's your nosegays of Mormons we're after having, Ludlow. We seen them shlipping in here!"

"It's shame to you, Ludlow, and your own dacent wife that hard to come at, by raison of King Strang!"

"Augh! thim bloomers!—they do be makin' me sthummick sick!"

"What hurts you worst," said Ludlow, "is the price you had to pay the Mormons for fish barrels."

The mob groaned and hooted. "Wull ye give us out the divil forninst there, or wull ye take a broadside through the windy?"

"I haven't any devil in the house."

"It's Jim Baker, be the powers. He wor seen, and his women."

"Jim Baker is here. But he's leaving the island at once with the women."

"He'll not lave it alive."

"You, Pat Corrigan," said Ludlow, pointing his finger at the torch-bearer, "do you remember the morning you and your mate rowed in to the light-house half-frozen and starved and I fed and warmed you?"

"Do I moind it? I do!"

"Did I let the Mormons take you then?"

"No, bedad."

"When King Strang's constables came galloping down here to arrest you, didn't I run in water to my waist to push you off in your boat?"

"You did, bedad!"

"I didn't give you up to them, and I won't give this family up to you. They're not doing you any harm. Let them peaceably leave Beaver."

"But the two wives of him," argued Pat Corrigan.

"How many wives and children have you?"

"Is it 'how many wives,' says the haythen! Wan wife, by the powers; and tin childer."

"Haven't you about as large a family as you can take care of?"

" Begobs, I have."

" Do you want to take in Jim Baker's Mormon wife and provide for her? Somebody has to. If you won't let him do it, perhaps you'll do it yourself."

" No, bedad !"

" Well, then, you'd better go about your business and let him alone. I don't see that we have to meddle with these things. Do you?"

The crowd moved uneasily and laughed, goodnaturedly owning to being plucked of its cause and arrested in the very act of returning evil for good.

" I tould you Ludlow was the foine man," said the torch-bearer to his confederates.

" There's no harm in you boys," pursued the fine man. " You're not making a war on women."

" We're not. Thrue for you."

" If you feel like having a wake over the Mormons, why don't you get more torches and make a procession down the Galilee road? You've done about all you can on Mount Pisgah."

As they began to trail away at this suggestion and to hail him with parting shouts, Ludlow shut the window and laughed in the dark room.

" I'd like to start them chasing the fox around all the five lakes on Beaver. But they may change their minds before they reach the sand-hills. We'd better load the boat right off, Jim."

In the hurrying Rosanne came down-stairs and found Elizabeth waiting at the foot. They could

see each other only by starlight. They were alone,
for the others had gone out to the boat.

" Are you willing for me to go, Rosanne?" spoke
Elizabeth. Her sweet voice was of a low pitch,
unhurried and steady. "James says he'll build me
a little house in your yard."

"Oh, Elizabeth!"

Rosanne did not cry, "I cannot hate you!" but
she threw herself into the arms of the larger, more
patient woman whom she saw no longer as a rival,
and who would cherish her children. Elizabeth
kissed her husband's wife as a little sister.

The lights on Beaver, sinking to duller redness,
shone behind Elizabeth like the fires of the stake as
she and Cecilia walked after the others to the boat.
Cecilia wondered if her spirit rose against the in-
dignities of her position as an undesired wife, whose
legal rights were not even recognized by the society
into which she would be forced. The world was
not open to her as to a man. In that day it would
have stoned her if she ventured too far from some
protected fireside. Fierce envy of squaws who
could tramp winter snows and were not despised
for their brief marriages may have flashed through
Elizabeth like the little self-protecting blaze a man
lighted around his own cabin when the prairie was
on fire. Why in all the swarming centuries of
human experience had the lot of a creature with
such genius for loving been cast where she was
utterly thrown away?

Solitary and carrying her passion a hidden coal

she walked in the footsteps of martyrs behind the pair of reunited lovers.

"Take care, Rosanne. Don't stumble, darling!" said the man to whom Elizabeth had been married by a law she respected until a higher law unhusbanded her.

Cecilia noted the passionate clutch of her hand and its withdrawal without touching him as he lurched over a rock.

He put his wife tenderly in the boat and then turned with kind formality to Elizabeth ; but Ludlow had helped her.

"Well, bon voyage," said the lighthouse-keeper. "Mind you run up the lantern on the mast as soon as you get aboard. I don't think there'll be any chase. The Irish have freed their minds."

"I'll send your fishing-boat back as soon as I can, Ludlow."

"Turn it over to father; he'll see to it. Give him news of us and our love to all the folks. He will be anxious to know the truth about Beaver."

"Good-bye, Elizabeth and Rosanne!"

"Good-bye, Cecilia!"

A grinding on pebbles, then the thump of adjusted oars and the rush of water on each side of a boat's course, marked the fugitives' progress towards the anchored smack.

Suspended on starlit waters as if in eternity, and watching the smoke of her past go up from a looted island, Elizabeth had the sense of a great company around her. The uninstructed girl from the little

kingdom of Beaver divined a worldful of souls waiting and loving in hopeless silence and marching re-
sistlessly as the stars to their reward. For there is
a development like the unfolding of a god for those
who suffer in strength and overcome.

A BRITISH ISLANDER*

WELL, I wish you could have been here in Mrs. Gunning's day. She was the oddest woman on Mackinac. Not that she exerted herself to attract attention. But she was such a character, and her manners were so astonishing, that she furnished perennial entertainment to the few families of us constituting island society.

She was an English woman, born in South Africa, and married to an American army surgeon, and had lived over a large part of the world before coming to this fort. She had no children. But her sister had married Dr. Gunning's brother. And the good-for-nothing pair set out to follow the English drum-beat around the world, and left a child for the two more responsible ones to rear. Juliana Gunning was so deaf she could not hear thunder. But she was quits with nature, for all that; a wonderfully alluring kind of girl, with big brown eyes that were better than ears, and that could catch the meaning of moving lips. It seemed to strangers

* This story is set down exactly as it was told by the Island Chronicler.

that she merely evaded conversation; for she had a
sweet voice, a little drawling, and was witty when
she wanted to speak. Juliana couldn't step out of
the surgeon's quarters to walk across the parade-
ground without making every soldier in the fort
conscious of her. She was well-shaped and tall,
and a slight pitting of the skin only enhanced the
charm of her large features. She used to dress unlike anybody else, in foreign things that her aunt
gave her, and was always carrying different kinds
of thin scarfs to throw over her face and tantalize
the men.

Everybody knew that Captain Markley would
marry her if he could. But along comes Dr. Mc-
Curdy, a wealthy widower from the East, and
nothing will do but he must hang about Mackinac week after week, pretending to need the climate
—and he weighing nearly two hundred—to court
Juliana Gunning. The lieutenant's wife said of
Juliana that she would flirt with a half-breed if
nothing better offered. But the lieutenant's wife
was a homely, jealous little thing, and could never
have had all the men hanging after her. And if
she had had the chance she might have been as aggravating about making up her mind between two
as Juliana was.

We used to think the girl very good-natured.
But those three people made a queer family. Dr.
Gunning was the remnant of a magnificent man,
and he always had a courtly air. He paid little
attention to the small affairs of life, and rated

money as nothing. Dr. Gunning had his peculiarities; but I am not telling you about him. He was a kind man, and would cross the strait in any weather to attend a sick half-breed or any other ailing creature, who probably never paid him a cent. He was fond of the island, and quite satisfied to spend his life here.

The day I am telling you about, Mrs. Gunning had driven with me into the village to make some calls. She was very punctilious about calling upon strangers. If she intended to recognize a newcomer she called at once. We drove around to the rear of the fort and entered at the back sally-port, where carriages always enter; but instead of letting me put her down at the surgeon's quarters, she ordered the driver to stop in the middle of the parade-ground. Then she got out and, with never a word, marched down the steps to Captain Markley, where he was leaning against the front sally-port, looking below into the town. I didn't know what to do, so I sat and waited. It was the loveliest autumn morning you ever saw. I remember the beeches and oaks and maples were spread out like banners to the very height of the island, all crimson and yellow splashes in the midst of evergreens. There had been an awful storm the night before, and you could see down the sally-port how drenched the fort garden was at the foot of the hill.

Captain Markley had a fearfully depressed look. He was so down in the mouth that the sentinels noticed it. I saw the one in front of the western block-house stick his tongue in his cheek and wink at one pacing below. We heard afterwards that Captain Markley had been out alone to inspect target-ranges in the pine woods, and almost ran against Juliana Gunning and Dr. McCurdy sitting on a log. Before he could get out of the way he overheard the loudest proposal ever made on Mackinac. It used to be told about in mess, though how it got out Captain Markley said he did not know, unless they heard it at the fort.

"I have brought you out here," the doctor shouted to Juliana, as loud as a cow lowing, "to tell you that I love you! I want you to be my wife!"

She behaved as if she didn't hear—I think that minx often had fun with her deafness—and inclined her head to one side.

So he said it all over again.

"I have brought you to this secluded spot to tell you that I love you! I want you to be my wife!"

It was like a steamer bellowing on the strait. Then Juliana threw her scarf over her face, and Captain Markley broke away through the bushes.

Mrs. Gunning never said a word to me about either of the suitors. It wasn't because she didn't talk, for she was a great talker. We had to postpone a card-party one evening, on account of the continuous flow of Mrs. Gunning's conversation, which never ceased until it was time for refreshments, there being not a moment's pause for the tables to be set out.

I WAS STARTLED TO SEE HER RUSH AT THE CAPTAIN

I was startled to see her rush down at Captain Markley, brandishing her parasol as if she were going to knock him down. I thought if she had any preference it would be for an army man; for you know an army woman's contempt of civilian money and position. Army women continually want to be moving on; and they hate bothering with household stuff, such as we prize.

Captain Markley did look poor-spirited, drooping against the sally-port, for a man who in his uniform was the most conspicuous figure to Mackinac girls in a ball-room. Maybe if he had been courting anything but a statue he might have made a better figure at it. Juliana was worse than a statue, though; for she could float through a thousand graceful poses, and drive a man crazy with her eyes. He wasn't the lover to go out in the woods and shoot a proposal as loud as a cannon at a girl; and it seems he couldn't get any satisfaction from her by writing notes.

Mrs. Gunning was drawing off her gloves as she marched at him with her parasol, and I remember how her emeralds and diamonds flashed in the sun —old heirlooms. I never saw another woman who had so many precious stones. She was tall, with that robust English quality that sometimes goes with slenderness. She and Juliana were not a bit alike. When she walked, her feet came down pat. I pitied Captain Markley. By leaning over the carriage I could see him give a start as Mrs. Gunning pounced at him.

"It's a fine day after the storm, Captain Markley," says she; and he lifted his cap and said it was.

Then she made a rush that I thought would drive him down the cliff, and whirled her parasol around his head like sword-play, talking about the havoc of the storm. She rippled him from head to foot and poked at his eyes, and jabbed him, to show how lightning struck the rocks, Captain Markley all the time moving back and dodging; and to save my life I couldn't help laughing, though the sentinels above him saw it. They were pretty well used to her, and rolled their quids in their cheeks, and winked at one another.

When she had all but thrown him down-hill, she stuck the ferrule right under his nose and shook it, and says she: "Yet it is now as fine a day as if no such convulsion had ever threatened the island. It is often so in this world."

He couldn't deny that, miserable as he looked. And I thought she would let him alone and come and say good-day to me. But no, indeed! She took him by the arm. Soldiers off duty were lounging on the benches, and Captain Markley wouldn't let them see him haled like a prisoner. He marched square-shouldered and erect; and Mrs. Gunning says to me as they reached the carriage:

"The captain will help you down if you will come with us. I am going to show him my Shanghai rooster."

I thanked her, and gladly let him help me down. I wasn't going to desert the poor fellow when Mrs.

Gunning was dealing with him; and, besides, I wanted to see that rooster myself. We heard such stories of the way she kept her chickens and labored over all the domestic animals she gathered around herself at the fort.

By ascending a steep bank on which the western block-house stands, you know you can look down into the drill-ground—that wide meadow behind the fort, with quarters at the back. Mrs. Gunning had an enclosure built outside the wall for her chickens; and there they were, walking about, scratching the ground, and diverting themselves as well as they could in their clothes. She had a shed at one end of the enclosure, and all the hens, walking about or sitting on nests, wore hoods! Holes were made for their eyes but none for their beaks, and the eyelets seemed to magnify so that they looked wrathy as they stretched their necks and quavered in those bags. Captain Markley and I both burst out laughing, but Mrs. Gunning explained it all seriously.

"They eat their eggs," says she; "so I tie hoods on them until I have collected the eggs for the day."

I remember some were clawing their head-gear, trying alternate feet, and two determined hens were trying to peck each other free. But they were generally resigned, and we might have grown so after the first minute, if it hadn't been for the rooster.

Captain Markley roared, and I leaned against the lower part of the block-house and held my sides. That long-legged, awkward, high-stepping Shanghai cock was dressed like a man in a suit of clothes—all but a hat. His coat-sleeves extended over his wings, and when he flapped them to crow, and stuck his claws out of his trousers-legs, I wept tears on my handkerchief. Mrs. Gunning talked straight ahead without paying any attention to our laughter. If it ever had been funny to her it had ceased to be so. She had not brought Captain Markley there to amuse him.

"Look at that Shanghai rooster now," says she. "I brought him up from the South. I put him among the hens and they picked all his feathers off. He was as bare, captain, as your hand. He was literally hen-pecked. First one would step up to him and pull out a feather; then another; and he, poor fool, did nothing but cower against the fence. It never seemed to enter his brain-pan he could put a stop to the torture. There he was, without a feather to cover himself with, and the cool autumn nights coming on. So I took some gray cloth and made him these clothes. He would have been picked to the bone if I hadn't. But they put spunk into him. That Shanghai rooster has found out he has to assert himself, captain, and he does assert himself."

I saw Captain Markley turn red, and I knew he wished the sentinel wasn't standing guard a few feet away in front of that block-house.

She might have let him alone after she had given him that thrust, and gone on to her house, and said

THE QUARTERS

good-bye in the usual way. But just as he was helping me down it happened that Juliana and Dr. McCurdy appeared through the rear sally-port, which they must have reached by skirting the wall instead of crossing the drill-field. As soon as Mrs. Gunning saw them she stiffened, and clubbed her umbrella at Captain Markley again. He couldn't get away, so he stood his ground.

"See that creature begin to curvet and roll her eyes!" says Mrs. Gunning. "If the parade-ground were full of men I think she would prance over the parapet. At my age she may have some sense and feeling. But I would be glad to see her in the hands of a man who knew how to assert himself."

"May I ask," says Captain Markley, "what you mean by a man's asserting himself, Mrs. Gunning?"

She made such a pounce at him with the parasol that her waist began to rip in the back.

"My dear boy, I am a full-blooded Briton, and Juliana is what you may call an English half-breed. In the bottom of our hearts we have a hankering for monarchy. The lion, who permits nobody else to poach on his preserves, is our symbol. While the vexatious child and I are not at all alike in other things, I know she admires as much as I do a man who asserts himself."

Though it was said Juliana Gunning could not hear thunder, she generally understood her aunt's voice, and could tell when she was being talked about. She came straight to her own rescue, as you might say, and Dr. McCurdy, poor man, was very polite, but not cheerful. If we had known then what he had been yelling in the woods, we should have understood better why Captain Markley seemed to pluck up and strut at the sight of him.

I think Mrs. Gunning determined to finish the business that very hour. She met Dr. McCurdy with all the sweetness she could put into her manner just before she intended to pounce the hardest.

" I have been showing the captain my chickens," she says, " and now I want to show you my cows."

Dr. McCurdy thanked her, and said he would be delighted to see the cows, but he stuck to Juliana like a shadow. Maybe he expected the cows would give him a further excuse for being with her. But Mrs. Gunning cut him off there. She gave her keys to her niece, and says she:

" Go in the house, my dear, and set out the decanter and glasses, and give Captain Markley a glass of wine to keep him until we come back. I want to tell him something more about that Shanghai rooster."

Juliana understood, and took the keys, and rolled her eyes tantalizingly at Dr. McCurdy. The poor fellow made a stand, and said the cows would do some other time, and mightn't he beg for a glass of wine too, after his walk?

" Certainly, doctor, certainly," says Mrs. Gunning, leading the way to the front sally-port. " We expect you to take a glass with us. But while Juliana sets out the decanter, let us look at the cows."

She hadn't mentioned me, but I didn't care for

that, knowing Mrs. Gunning as I did. I should have followed if she hadn't beckoned to me, for I was as determined to see the affair through as she was to finish it.

We had to go down that long path from the front sally-port to the street, and then turn into the field at the foot of the hill, where the fort stables are. Mrs. Gunning talked all the time about cattle, flourishing her parasol and flashing her diamonds and emeralds in the sun, and telling Dr. McCurdy she had intended to ask his opinion about them ever since his arrival on the island. He answered yes, and no, and seemed to be thinking of anything but cattle.

Mackinac cows tinkled their bells in every thicket. But Mrs. Gunning's pets were brought in morning and afternoon to clean, well-lighted stalls. There they stood in a row, sleek as if they had been curried—and I have heard that she did curry them herself — all switching natural tails except one. And, as sure as you live, that cow had a false tail that Mrs. Gunning had made for her!

She took hold of it and showed it to us. It did not seem very funny to Dr. McCurdy, but he had to listen to what she said.

"Spotty was a fine cow, but by some accident she had lost her tail, and I got her cheaper on that account," says Mrs. Gunning. "You don't know how distressing it was to see her switching a stump. So I made her a tail of whalebone and India-rubber and yarn. I knit it myself."

The poor fellow looked up at the fort and said: "Yes. It is very interesting, Mrs. Gunning."

"I am aware," says she, "that the expedient was never hit upon before. But Spotty's brush is a great success. It used to make me unhappy to think of leaving this post. All the other cows might find good homes with new owners; but who would care for Spotty? Since I have supplied her deficiency, however, and know that the supply can constantly be renewed, my mind is easy about her. If you ever have to knit a cow's tail, doctor, remember the foundations are whalebone and India-rubber; and I would advise you to use the coarsest yarn you can find for the brush."

"I will, Mrs. Gunning," he says, like a man who wanted to lie down in the straw and die. And I couldn't laugh and relieve myself, because it was like laughing at him.

"Now that shows," says Mrs. Gunning, and she pounced at him and shook her parasol in his face so vigorously that she ripped in the back the same as a chrysalis, "how easy it is to remedy a seemingly incurable injury."

If he didn't understand her then, he did afterwards. But he looked as if he couldn't endure it any longer, and made for the door.

"Stop, Dr. McCurdy," says she. "You haven't heard these cows' pedigrees."

He stopped, and said: "How long are the pedigrees?"

"Here are four generations," says Mrs. Gunning—
"grandmother, mother, daughter, and grandchild."
And on she went, tracing their lineage through
blooded stock for more than half an hour. She
was enthusiastic, too, and got between the doctor
and the door, and emphasized all her points with
the parasol. Her back kept ripping until I ought
to have told her, but I knew the man was too mad
to look at her, and she was so happy herself, I said,
" I will let her alone."

I had forgotten all about my half-breed driver,
sitting on the parade-ground in the waiting carriage. But he was enjoying himself too, when we
climbed to the fort again, with a soldier lounging
on the front wheel.

Well, as soon as I entered the little parlor that
Mrs. Gunning called her drawing-room—ornamented with the movable knickknacks that an army
woman carries around with her, you know—I saw
that Captain Markley had asserted himself. If he
hadn't asserted himself on that occasion, I do believe Mrs. Gunning would have been done with him
forever. I never saw a man so anxious to show
that he was accepted. Of course he couldn't announce the engagement until it had been sanc-
tioned by the girl's foster-parents. But he put Juliana through the engaged drill like a veteran, and
she was wonderfully meek.

I suppose one British woman knows another better than an American can. But I felt sorry for
Dr. McCurdy when he saw the state of things and

took his leave, and Mrs. Gunning rubbed his defeat on the raw.

"Ah, my dear friend," says she, shaking his hand, "we see that buds will match with buds. I could never find it in my heart to wed a bud to a full-blown rose."

I don't doubt that the full-blown rose, as he went down the fort hill, cursed Mrs. Gunning's cow's tail and all her cows' pedigrees. But she looked as serene as if he had pledged the young couple's health (instead of going off and leaving his wine half tasted), and took me to see her chickens' cupboard.

There were shelves with rows of cans and bottles, each can or bottle labelled "Molly," or "Lucy," or "Speckie," and so on.

"I have discovered," Mrs. Gunning says to me, "that one hen's food may be another hen's poison, so I mix and prepare for each fowl what that fowl seems to need. For instance, Lucy can bear more meal than Speckie, and the Shanghai cock had to be strongly encouraged. Though it sometimes happens," says she, casting her eye back towards the drawing-room, "that such a fellow gets pampered, and has to have his diet reduced and his spirit cooled down again."

THE CURSED PATOIS

AS his boat shot to the camp dock of beach
stones, the camper thought he heard a
child's voice behind the screen of brush.
He leaped out and drew the boat to its landing
upon a cross-piece held by two uprights in the
water, and ascended the steep path worn in leaf
mould.

There was not only a child, there was a woman
also in the camp. And Frank Puttany, his German feet planted outward in a line, his smiling
dark face unctuous with hospitality towards creatures whom he had evidently introduced, in foolish
helplessness gave his partner the usual greeting:

"Vell, Prowny."

"Hello, Puttany. Visitors?"

Brown pulled off his cap to the woman. She
was pretty, with eyes like a deer's, with white
teeth showing between her parted scarlet lips, and
much curling hair pinned up and blowing over her
ears. She had the rich tint of a quarter-breed,
lightened in her case by a constant suffusion which
gave her steady color. She was dressed in a mixt-
ure of patches, but all were fitted to her perfect

151

shape with a Parisian elegance sensed even by backwoodsmen. Pressed against her knee stood the dirtiest and chubbiest four-year-old child on the borders of Brevoort Lake—perhaps the dirtiest on the north shore of Michigan. The Indian mixed with his French had been improved on by the sun until he was of a brick redness and hardness of flesh; a rosy-meated thing, like a good muskalonge. Brown suddenly remembered the pair. They were Joe La France's wife and child. Joe La France was dead. Puttany had recently told him that Joe La France left a widow and a baby without shelter, and without relations nearer than Canada.

After greeting Brown the guest resumed her seat on one of the camp-chairs, a box worn smooth by much use, having a slit cut in the top through which the hand could be thrust to lift it.

The camp, in a small clearing, consisted of two tents, both of the wedge-shaped kind. The sleeping-tent was nearly filled by the bed it contained; and this, lifted a few inches above the ground on pole supports, was of browse or brush and straw, covered with blankets. A square canopy of mosquito-netting protected it. The cooking-tent had a foundation of logs and a canvas top. The floor was of pure white sand. Boxes like lockers were stored under the eaves to hold food, and in one corner a cylindrical camp-stove with an oven thrust its pipe through a tinned hole in the roof. Plenty of iron skillets, kettles, and pans hung above the lockers on pegs in the logs; and the camp dinner service of white ware, black-handled knives and forks, and metal spoons, neatly washed, stood on a table. Jess, the Scotch collie, who was always left to guard the tents in their owners' absence, sat at her usual post within the door; and she and Brown exchanged repressed growls at the strangers. Jess, being freed from her chain, trotted at his heels when he went back to the beach to clean fish for supper. She sat and watched his deft and work-hardened hands as he dipped and washed and drew and scaled his spoil. He was a clean-skinned, blue-eyed Canadian Irishman, well made and sinewy, bright and open of countenance. His blond hair clung in almost flaxen tendrils to his warm forehead. No ill-nature was visible about him, yet he turned like a man in fierce self-defence on his partner, who followed Jess and stood also watching him.

"Puttany, you fool! what have you brought these cursed patois into camp for?"

"Joe La France vas my old pardner," softly pleaded the German.

"Damn you, man, we can't start an orphan-asylum and widows' home! We'll get a bad name at the hotels. The real good people won't have us for guides."

"She told me in Allanville she had no place to stay. She did not know what to do. At the old voman's, where Joe put her, they have need of her bed. The old voman is too poor to keep her any more."

"I'd have done just what you did; that's what makes me so mad. How long is she going to stay?"

"I don't know," sheepishly responded his partner.

"A Dutchman ought to have more sense than to load up with a lot of cursed patois. Nothing but French and Indian! We'll have to put the precious dears in the sleeping-tent, and bunk down ourselves with blankets in the other. Did you air the blankets good this morning, Frank?"

"They vos vell aired."

"You're a soft mark, Frank! One of us will have to marry Joe La France's widow—that's what it will come to!" Brown slapped the water in violent disgust, but Puttany blushed a dark and modest red.

Men of their class rarely have vision or any kind of foresight. They live in the present and plan no farther than their horizon, being, like children, overpowered by visible things. But the Irish Canadian had lived many lives as lake sailor and lumberman, and he had a shrewd eye and quick humor. It was he who had devised the conveniences of the camp, and who delicately and skilfully prepared the meals so that the two fared like epicures; while Puttany did the scullery-work, and was superior only at deerstalking.

The perfume of coffee presently sifted abroad, and the table was brought out and set under the evening sky. Lockers gave up their store of bread and pastry made by the capable hands of the camp housekeeper. The woman, their guest, sat watching him move from cook-tent to table, and Puttany lounged on the dog-kennel, whittling a stick.

"Frank," said his partner, with sudden authority, "you take the kid down to the water and scrub him."

"All over?" whispered Puttany, in confusion.

"No—just his hands and top. Supper is ready to put on."

The docile mother heard her child yelling and blubbering under generous douches while nurse's duty was performed by one of her entertainers, and she smiled in proof that her faith was grounded on their righteousness. She was indeed a mere girl. Her short scarlet upper lip showed her teeth with piquant innocence. As much a creature of the woods as a doe, her lot had been that primitive struggle which knows nothing about the amenities and proprieties of civilization. This Brown could clearly see, and he addressed her with the same protecting patronage he would have used with the child.

"What's your kid's name?"

"Grégoire, but he call himself Gougou. Me, I am Françoise La France."

"Yes, I know that. You have had a hard time since Joe died."

"I been anxion"—she clasped her hands and looked pleadingly at him—"I been very anxion!"

"Well, you're all right now."

" You let me do de mend'? I can sew. I use' learn to sew when I have t'ing to sew on."

" Jerusalem! look at them shirts on the line! We have more clothes to sew on than any dude at the hotels. And if that isn't enough, I'll make Puttany strip and stay in the brush while you do his clothes."

Françoise widened her smile.

" I've been thinking we'll have to build you a house right over there." Her entertainer indicated the shore behind her.

" Oppos'?" exclaimed Françoise, turning with pleased interest. Even in her husband's lifetime little thought had ever been taken for her.

" Yes, directly opposite. We can fix it up snug like our winter camp at the other end of the lake."

" Have you two camp?"

" Yes—a winter camp and a summer camp. But we have stayed comfortably here in the cook-tent until the thermometer went fourteen degrees below zero. We'll sleep in it till we get your house done, and you can take the tent. If there are no parties wanting guides, we might as well begin it in the morning."

" But," faltered Françoise, "afterw'iles when de ice is t'ick, and you go to de hudder camp—"

" Oh, we'll take care of you," he promised. "You and Gougou will go with us. We couldn't leave you on this side."

" In de dark nights," shuddered Françoise.

" You needn't be afraid, any time. When we

are off during the day we always leave Jess and
Jim to guard the camp. Jess is a Scotch collie and
Jim is a blood-hound. He's there in the kennel.
Neither man nor varmint would have any chance
with them."

"I been use' to live alone when my husban' is
away, M'sieu' Brownee. I not 'fraid like you t'ink.
But if Gougou be cold and hongry."

"Now that's enough," said Brown, with gentle
severity. "Gougou will never be cold and hungry
again while there's a stick of wood to be cut on the
shores of this lake, or any game to bag, or a 'lunge
to spear through the ice. We get about two days'
lumbering a week down by St. Ignace. No use to
work more than two days a week," he explained,
jocosely. "That gives us enough to live on; and
everybody around here owes us from fifty to a
hundred dollars back pay for work, anyhow. I've
bought this ground, twenty acres of it, and another
year I'm going to turn it into a garden."

"Oh, a garden, M'sieu' Brownee! Me, I love
some garden! I plant honion once, salade also."

"But I want to get my fences built before I put
in improvements. You know what the silver rule
is, don't you?"

"No, m'sieu'," answered Françoise, vaguely.
She knew little of any rule.

"The silver rule is different from the golden rule.
It's 'Do your neighbors, or your neighbors will do
you.' If I don't protect myself, all the loose cattle
around Brevoort will graze over me. Every fellow

for himself. We can't keep the golden rule. We'd never get rich if we did."

"You are rich mans?" interrogated Françoise, focussing her curiosity on that invisible power of wealth.

"Millionaires," brazenly claimed the young man, as he put an earthen-ware pitcher on the table. "Set there, you thousand-dollar dish! We don't have a yacht on the lake because we prefer small boats, and we go out as guides to have fun with the greenhorns. The cooking at the hotels is good enough for common hunters and fishermen who come here from the cities to spend their money, but it isn't good enough for me. You've come to the right place, you may make your mind easy on that."

Françoise smiled because he told her to make her mind easy, not because she understood the irony of his poverty. To have secure shelter, and such a table as he spread, and the prowess to achieve continual abundant sustenance from the world, made wealth in her eyes. She was as happy as Gougou when this strange family, gathered from three or four nations, sat down to their first meal.

The sun went low like a scarlet egg, probing the mother-of-pearl lake with a long red line of shadow, until it wasted into grayness and so disappeared. Then home-returning sails became spiritualized, and moved in mist as in a dream—foggy lake and sky, as one body, seeming to push in upon the land.

Françoise slept the sleep of a healthy woman,

with her child on her arm, until at dawn the closed
flap of the tent yielded to a bounding shape. She
opened her startled eyes to see Jim the blood-hound
at the foot of the bed, jerking the mosquito-netting.
He growled at the interlopers, not being able in his
canine mind to reconcile their presence with his
customary duty of waking his masters in that tent.
A call and a whistle at the other side of the camp
drew him away doubting. But in a day both he
and Jess had adopted the new members of the family
and walked at Gougou's heels.

Gougou existed in wonderland. He regarded the
men as great and amiable powers, who could do
what they pleased with the elements and with the
creatures of the earth. They had a fawn, which
had followed Brown home along the beach, feeding
on leaves from his hand. They had built it a sylvan
home of cedar boughs behind the camp, from which
it wandered at will. And though at first shy of
Gougou, the pretty thing was soon induced to stand
upon its hind feet and dance for bits of cake. His
Indian blood yearned towards the fawn; but Methuselah, the mighty turtle, was more exciting.
Methuselah lived a prisoner in one side of the bait-
tank, from which he was lifted by a rope around
his tail. He was so enormous that it required both
Brown and Puttany to carry him up the bank, and
as he hung from the pole the sudden projection of
his snapping head was a danger. When he fastened
his teeth into a stick, the stick was hopelessly his
as long as he chose to keep it. He was like an

elephant cased in mottled shell, and the serrated ridge on his tail resembled a row of huge brown teeth. Methuselah was a many-wrinkled turtle. When he contracted, imbedding head in shoulders and legs in body, revealing all his claws and showing wicked little eyes near the point of his nose, his helpless rage stirred all the Indian; he was the most deliciously devilish thing that Gougou had ever seen.

Then there was the joy of wintergreen, which both men brought to the child, and he learned to forage for it himself. The fleshy dark green leaves and red berries clustered thickly in the woods. He and his mother went in the boat when the day was to be given to bass or pickerel fishing, and he learned great lessons of water-lore from the two men. If they trusted a troll line to his baby hands, he was in a state of beatitude. His object in life was to possess a bear cub, and many a porcupine creeping along the beach he mistook for that desirable property, until taught to distinguish quills from fur. Gougou heard, and he believed, that all porcupines were old lumbermen, who never died, but simply contracted to that shape. He furtively stoned them when he could, reflecting that they were tough, and delighting to see the quills fly.

Françoise would sit in the camp like a picture of still life, glowing and silent at her appointed labor. She sewed for all of them, looking womanly and unhurried, with a pink-veined moccasin-flower in her hair; while Brown, cooking and baking, rushed

from tent to wood-pile, his sleeves turned back from
his white, muscular arms. He lived more intensely
than any other member of the sylvan household.
His blue eyes shone, and his face was vivid as he
talked to her. He was a common man, blunted in
the finer nature by a life of hardship, yet his shrewd
spirit seized on much that less facile people like
Puttany learned slowly or not at all.

Puttany and the child were often together in one
long play, broken only by the man's periods of
labor. They basked in a boat near rushes, waiting
for pickerel to strike, or waded a bog to a trout
stream at the other end of the lake, hid in a forest
full of windfalls and hoary moss and tropical
growths of brake and fern. Gougou had new strong
clothes and buckskin shoes. For the patois had
not been a week in camp before Brown went to St.
Ignace and brought back denim and white and
black calico, which he presented to Françoise.

"She ought to have a kind of second mourning,"
he explained to Puttany, who received his word on
any matter as law. "Joe La France wasn't worth
wearing first mourning for, but second mourning is
decent for her, and it won't show in the camp like
bright colors would."

The world of city-maddened people who swarmed
to this lake for their annual immersion in nature
did not often intrude on the camp. Yet the fact of
a woman's presence there could not be concealed,
and Puttany was disciplined to say to strangers,
"Dot vas my sister and her little poy."

A tiny cabin was built for Françoise, with the luxuries of a puncheon floor and one glazed window. She inhabited it in primitive gladness, as a child adorns a play-house, and was careful to keep it in that trim, military state which Brown demanded. Françoise had a regard for M'sieu' Puttanee, who was neat and ladylike in all his doings, and smiled amiably at her over her boy's head; but her veneration of M'sieu' Brownee extended beyond the reach of humor. If he had been a priest he could have had no more authority. She used to watch him secretly from her window at dawn, as he put himself through a morning drill to limber his muscles. Some spectators might have laughed, but she heard as seriously as if they were the motions of her own soul his tactics with a stick:

"Straight out—across the shoulder—under the arm—down on the turf!"

There were days when the misty gray lake, dim and delicious, lay veiled within its irregular shores. Then the lowering sun stood on tree-tops, a pale red wraith like the ghost of an Indian. And there were days of sharp, clear shine, when Black Point seemed to approach across the water, and any moving object could be seen in the Burning—a growth of green springing where the woods had been swept by fire. The men were often away, guiding fishing parties from dawn until sunset, or hunting parties from sunset half the night. Françoise and Gougou dwelt in the camp, having the dogs as their protectors, though neither primitive nor civilized life menaced them there with any danger. Some evenings, when few affairs had crowded the day, Brown sat like a patriarch in the midst of his family, and took Gougou on his knee to hear bear stories. He supervised the youngster's manners like a mother, and Gougou learned to go down to the washing-place and use soap when the signs were strong for bear-dens and deer-stalking.

"I saw a bear come out on the beach once," Brown would tell him, "when I was stalking for deer and had a doe and fawn in the lake. I smelt him, but couldn't get him to turn his eyes towards me. I killed both deer, and skinned them, and cut up one. And that bear went into the woods and howled for hours. I took all the venison I could carry, but left part of the carcasses. When we went after them in the morning, the bear had eaten all up clean."

Bear-dens, Gougou was informed, might be found where there was a windfall. The bears stuffed cracks between the fallen trees with moss, and so made themselves a tight house in which to hibernate. If you were obliged to have bear meat that season when the game was thin, you could cut a hole into a den, stand by it with an axe, and lop off the inquiring head stuck out to investigate disturbances. Bears had very small stomachs, but whatever they ate went to fat. They walked much on their hind feet, and browsed on nuts or mast when their hunting was not successful, being able to thrive on little. Usually a father, a mother, and a cub formed one household in one den.

Brown's mind ran on the subject of households; and he sometimes talked to Françoise about his mother.

"My mother Gaelics like the Scotch," he said. Françoise could not imagine what it was to Gaelic. People had not Gaelic-ed on the Chaudière, where she was brought up until the children were obliged to scatter from the narrow farm. But the priest had never warned her against it, and since M'sieu' Brownee's mother was addicted to the practice, it must be something excellent, perhaps even religious. She secretly invoked St. Francis, her patron saint, to obtain for her that mysterious power of Gaelic-ing of which M'sieu' Brownee spoke so tenderly.

So the summer passed, and frost was already ripening to glory the ranks on ranks of dense forest pressing to the lake borders. Brown and Puttany rowed home through an early September evening, lifted their boat to its cross-piece dock, and pulled the plug out of the bottom to let it drain. There was no sound, even of the dogs, as they flung their spoil ashore. It was the very instant of moon-rise. At first a copper rim was answered by the faintest line in the water. Then the full reddish disk stood upon a strong copper pillar, smooth and flawless in a rippleless lake, and that became denuded of its capital as the ball rose over it into the sky.

"Seems still," remarked Brown, and he ran up the path, shaking leaf loam like dry tobacco dust from the roots of ferns he had brought to Françoise. He knew at once that she and Gougou had left the camp. He sat down on the dog-kennel with his hands on his knees, staring at the dim earth. Puttany went from tent to cabin, calling his daily playmate, unable to convince himself that some unusual thing had happened, and he hoped that Brown would contradict him when he felt compelled to announce his slow discovery.

" Dey vas gone!"

" Damn you, Puttany!" exploded his partner, " what did you bring her here for? I didn't want to get into this! I wanted to steer clear of women! You knew I was soft! You knew her black eyes, and the child that made her seem like the Virgin, would get in their work on me!"

" No, I didn't," said Puttany, in phlegmatic consternation.

"What's the matter, Frank? Haven't we behaved white to this woman? Have you done anything, you stupid old Dutchman," cried Brown, collaring his partner with abrupt violence, " that would drive her out of the camp without a word?"

"I svear, Prowny," the other gasped, as soon as he had breath for swearing, "I haf been so polite to her as my own mudder."

The younger man sat down again, dropping lax hands across his knees. A growl inside the box reminded him that Jim the blood-hound should be brought to account for this disappearance.

"Come out here!" he commanded, and the lithe

165

beast crept wagging and apologizing to his side.
" What kind of a way is this for you to keep a camp
—Jess sitting in the kitchen, and you in the box,
and somebody carrying off Françoise and the boy,
and every rag that would show they had ever been
here—and not a sound out of your cowardly head
till we come home and catch you skulking? I've a
notion to take a board and beat you to death!"

Jim lay down with an abject and dismal whine.

" Where is she?"

Jim lifted his nose and sniffed hopefully, and his
master rose up and dragged him by the collar to
the empty cabin. It was the first time Brown had
entered that little cell since its dedication to the
woman for whom it was built. He rubbed Jim's
muzzle against the bed, and pointed to nails in the
logs where the clothes of the patois had hung.

"Now you lope out and find them — do you
hear?"

Jim, crouching on his belly in acknowledgment
that his apprehension had been at fault during some
late encounter, slunk across the camp and took the
path to the hotels.

Brown turned on Puttany following at his heels:
" Frank, are you sure Joe La France is dead?"

" Oh yes, he is det."

" Did you see him die? Were you there when
he was buried? Was he put underground with
plenty of dirt on top of him, or did he merely drop
in the water?"

" I vas not there."

"Maybe the lazy hound has resurrected. I've seen these lumbermen dropped into the water and drowned too often. You can never be sure they won't be up drinking and fighting to-morrow unless you run a knife through them."

"He is a det man," affirmed Puttany.

"Then somebody else has carried her off, and I'm going to know all about it before I come back to camp. If I never come back, you may have the stuff and land. I'm in this heels over head, and I don't care how soon things end with me."

"But, Prowny, old poy, I vill help you—"

"You stay here. This is my hunt."

Jim passed the rustic guest-houses without turning aside from the trail. Brown took no thought of inquiring at their doors, for throughout the summer Françoise had not once been seen at the hotels. He did, however, hastily borrow a horse from the stable where he was privileged, and pursuing the blood-hound along the lake shore, he cantered over a causeway of logs and earth which had been raised above a swamp.

The trail was very fresh, for Jim, without swerving, followed the road where it turned at right angles from the shore and wound inland among stumps. They had nearly reached Allanville, a group of log huts beside a north-shore railroad, when Jim uttered the bay of victory.

Brown dropped from the saddle and called him sternly back. To be hunting Françoise with a blood-hound out of leash—how horrible was this!

He tied his horse to a tree and took Jim by the collar, restraining the creature's fierce joy of discovery. Françoise must be near, unless a hound whose scent was unerring had become a fool.

What if she had left camp of her own will? She was so quiet, one could not be sure of her thoughts. Brown was sure of his thoughts. He grinned in the lonely landscape, seeing himself as he had appeared on recent Sundays, in his best turtle-tail neck-tie mounted on velvet.

"I've got it bad," he confessed.

Stooping to Jim's collar while the dog whined and strained, he passed a cabin. And there Jim relaxed in the search and turned around. The moon stood high enough to make a wan fairy daylight. Gougou, like a gnome, started from the ground to meet them, and the dog at once lay down and fawned at his feet.

More slowly approaching from the cabin, Brown saw Françoise, still carrying in her hand the bundle of her belongings brought from camp. In the shadow of the house a man watched the encounter, and a sift of rank tobacco smoke hinted the pipes of fathers and sons resting from the day's labor on the cabin door-sill or the sward. Voices of children could be heard, and other dogs gave mouth, so that Brown laid severe commands on Jim before he could tremblingly speak to Françoise.

"Oh, M'sieu' Brownee, I t'ink maybe you come!"

"But, Françoise, what made you leave?"

"It is my husban's brudder. I not know what

to do! He bring us to dese folks to stay all night till de cars go."

"Why didn't he show himself to us, and take you like a man?"

"Oh, M'sieu' Brownee—he say de priest hexcommunicate me—to live—so—in de camp! It is not my fault—and I t'ink about you and M'sieu' Puttanee—and Gougou he bite his honcle, and kick and scream!"

"Damn the uncle!" swore Brown, deeply.

"Oh, I been so anxion!" sobbed Françoise.

"We must be married right off," said Brown. "I'll fix your brother-in-law. Françoise, will you have me for your husband?"

"Me, M'sieu' Brownee?"

"Yes, you—you cursed sweet patois!"

"M'sieu' Brownee, you may call me de cursed patois. I not know anyt'ings. But when André La France take me away, oh, I t'ink I die! Let me honly be Françoise to do your mend'! I be 'appier to honly look at you dan some womans who 'ave 'usban'!"

"Françoise, kiss me—kiss me!" His voice broke with a sob. "If you loved me you would have me!"

"M'sieu' Brownee, I ado' you!"

Suddenly giving way to passionate weeping, and to all the tenderness which nature teaches even barbarians to repress, she abandoned herself to his arms.

THE MOTHERS OF HONORÉ

THE sun was shining again after squalls, and
the strait showed violet, green, red, and
bronze lines, melting and intermingling each
changing second. Metallic lustres shone as if some
volcanic fountain on the lake-bed were spraying the
surface. Jules McCarty stood at his gate, noting
this change in the weather with one eye. He was
a small, old man, having the appearance of a mum-
mied boy. His cheek-bones shone apple-red, and
his partial blindness had merely the effect of a prolonged wink. Jules was keeping melancholy holi-
day in his best clothes, the well-preserved coat
parting its jaunty tails a little below the middle of
his back.

Another old islander paused at the gate in passing. The two men shook their heads at each
other.

"I went to your wife's funeral this morning,
Jules," said the passer, impressing on the widower's
hearing an important fact which might have escaped
his one eye.

"You was at de funer'l? Did you see Therese?"

"Yes, I saw her."

"Ah, what a fat woman dat was! I make some of de peop' feel her arm. I feed her well."

The other old man smiled, but he was bound to say,

"I'm sorry for you, Jules."

"Did you see me at de church?"

"Yes, I went to the church."

"You t'ink I feel bad—eh?"

"I thought you felt pretty bad."

"You go to de graveyard, too?"

"No," admitted his sympathizer, reluctantly, "I didn't go to the graveyard."

"But dat was de fines'. You ought see me at de graveyard. You t'ink I feel bad at de church—I raise hell at de graveyard."

The friend shuffled his feet and coughed behind his hand.

"Yes, I feel bad, me," ruminated the bereaved man. "You get used to some woman in de house and not know where to get anodder."

"Haven't you had your share, Jules?" inquired his friend, relaxing gladly to banter.

"I have one fine wife, maman to Honoré," enumerated Jules, "and de squaw, and Lavelotte's widow, and Therese. It is not much."

"I've often wondered why you didn't take Melinda Cree. You've no objection to Indians. She's next door to you, and she knows how to nurse in sickness, besides being a good washer and ironer. The summer folks say she makes the best fish pies on the island."

"It is de trut'!" exclaimed Jules, a new light shining in his dim blue eye as he turned it towards the house of Melinda Cree. The weather-worn, low domicile was bowered in trees. There was a convenient stile two steps high in the separating fence, and it had long been made a thoroughfare by the families. On the top step sat Clethera, Melinda Cree's granddaughter. Clethera had been Honoré's playmate since infancy. She was a lithe, dark girl, with more of her French father in her than of her half-breed mother. Some needle-work busied her hands, but her ear caught every accent of the conference at the gate. She flattened her lips, and determined to tell Honoré as soon as he came in with the boat. Honoré was the favorite skipper of the summer visitors. He went out immediately after the funeral to earn money to apply on his last mother's burial expenses.

When the old men parted, Clethera examined her grandmother with stealthy eyes in a kind of aboriginal reconnoitring. Melinda Cree's black hair and dark masses of wrinkles showed through a sashless shed window where she stood at her ironing-board. Her stoical eyelids were lowered, and she moved with the rhythmical motion of the smoothing-iron. Whether she had overheard the talk, or was meditating on her own matrimonial troubles, was impossible to gather from facial muscles rigid as carved wood. Melinda Cree was one of the few pure-blooded Indians on the island. If she was fond of anything in the world, her preference had not declared itself, though previous to receiving her orphaned granddaughter into her house she had consented to become the bride of a drunken youth in his teens. This incipient husband—before he got drowned in a squall off Detour, thereby saving his aged wife some outlay—visited her only when he needed funds, and she silently paid the levy if her toil had provided the means. He also inclined to offer delicate attentions to Clethera, who spat at him like a cat, and at sight of him ever afterwards took to the attic, locking the door.

But while Melinda Cree submitted to the shackles of civilization, she did not entirely give up the ways of her own people. She kept a conical tent of poles and birch bark in her back yard, in which she slept during summer. And she was noted as wise and skilled in herbs, guarding their secrets so jealously that the knowledge was likely to die with her. Once she appeared at the bedside of a dying islander, and asked, as the doctor had withdrawn, to try her own remedies. Permission being given, she went to the kitchen, took some dried vegetable substance from her pocket, and made a tea of it. A little was poured down the sick man's throat. He revived. He drank more, and grew better. Melinda Cree's decoction cured him, and the chagrined doctor visited her to learn what wonderful remedy she had used.

"It was nothing but some little bushes," responded the Indian woman.

"If you tell me what they are, I will pay you fifty dollars," he pleaded.

Melinda Cree shook her head. She continued to repeat, as he raised the bid higher, "It was nothing but some little bushes, doctor; it was nothing but some little bushes."

Clethera felt the same kind of protecting tenderness for this self-restrained squaw that Honoré had for his undersized parent, whom he always called by the baptismal name. Melinda had been the wife of a great medicine-man, who wore a trailing blanket, and white gulls' wings bound around and spread behind his head. During his lifetime he was often seen stretched on his back invoking the sun. A stranger observing him declared he was using the signs of Freemasonry, and must know its secrets.

With the readiness of custom, Honoré and Clethera met each other at the steps in the fence about dusk. She sat down on her side, and he sat down on his, the broad top of the stile separating them. Honoré was a stalwart Saxon-looking youth in his early twenties. Wind and weather had painted his large-featured countenance a rosy tan. By the employing class Honoré was considered one of the finest and most promising young quarter-breeds on the island.

The fresh moist odor of the lake, with its incessant wash upon pebbles, came to them accompanied by piercing sweetness of wild roses. For the wind had turned to the west, raking fragrant thickets. Dusk was moving from eastern fastnesses to rock battlements still tinged with sunset. The fort, dismantled of its garrison, reared a whitewashed crown against the island's back of evergreens.

Both Honoré and Clethera knew there was a Spanish war. As summer day followed summer day, the village seethed with it, as other spots then seethed. A military post, even when dismantled, always brings home to the community where it is situated the dignity and pomp of arms. Young men enlisted, and Honoré restlessly followed, with a friend from the North Shore, to look at the camp. His pulses beat with the drums. But he was carrying the burden of the family; to leave Jules and Jules's dependent wife would be deserting infants.

Clethera gave little more thought to fleets sailing tropical seas than to La Salle's vanished *Griffin* on Northern waters. It was nothing to her, for she had never heard of it, that pioneers of her father's blood once trod that island, and lifted up the cross at St. Ignace, and planted outposts along the South Shore. Bareheaded, or with a crimson kerchief bound about her hair, she loved to help her grandmother spread the white clothes to bleach, or to be seen and respected as a prosperous laundress carrying her basket through the teeming streets. The island was her world. Its crowds in summer brought variety enough; and its virgin winter snows, the dog-sledges, the ice-boats, were month by month a procession of joys.

Clethera wondered that Honoré persistently went where newspapers were read and discussed. He stuffed them in his pockets, and pored over them while waiting in his boat beside the wharf. People would fight out that war with Spain. What thrilled her was the boom of winter surf, piling iridescent frozen spume as high as a man's head, and rimming the island in a corona of shattered rainbows. And she had an eye for summer lightning infusing itself through sheets of water as if descending in the downpour, glorifying for one instant every distinct drop.

The pair sitting with the broad top step betwixt them exchanged the smiling good-will of youth.

"I take some more party out to-night for de light-moon sail," said Honoré, pleased to report his prosperity. "It is consider' gran' to sail in de light-moon."

"Did you find de hot fish pie?" inquired Clethera, solicitous about man thrown on his own resources as cook.

Honoré acknowledged with hearty gratitude the supper which Melinda Cree had baked and her granddaughter had carried into the bereaved house while its inmates were out.

"They not get fish pie like that in de war. Jules, he say it is better than poor Therese could make," Honoré added, handsomely, with large unsuspicion.

Clethera shook a finger in his face.

"Honoré McCarty, you got watch dat Jules! I got to watch Melinda. Simon Leslie, he have come by and put it in Jules' head since de funer'l! I hear it, me."

The young man's face changed through the dusk.

He braced his back against the fence and breathed the deep sigh of tried patience.

"Honoré, how many mothers is it you have already?"

"I have not count'," said the young man, testily.

"Count dem mothers," ordered Clethera.

"Maman," he began the enumeration, reverently. His companion allowed him a minute's silence after the mention of that fine woman.

"One," she tallied.

"Nex'," proceeded Honoré, "poor Jules is involve' with de Chippewa woman."

"Two," clinched Clethera.

The Chippewa squaw was a sore theme. She had entered Jules's wigwam in good faith; but during one of his merry carouses, while both Honoré and the priest were absent, he traded her off to a North Shore man for a horse. Long after she tramped away across the frozen strait with her new possessor, and all trace of her was lost, Jules had the grace to be shamefaced about the scandal; but he got a good bargain in the horse.

"Then there is Lavelotte's widow," continued Honoré.

"Three," marked Clethera.

Yes, there was Lavelotte's widow, the worst of all. She whipped little Jules unmercifully, and if Honoré had not taken his part and stood before him, she might have ended by being Jules's widow. She stripped him of his whole fortune, four hundred dollars, when he finally obtained a separation from her. But instead of curing him, this experience only whetted his zest for another wife.

"And there is Therese." Honoré did not say, "Last, Therese." While Jules lived and his wives died, or were traded off or divorced, there would be no last.

"It is four," declared Clethera; and the count was true. Honoré had taken Jules in hand like a father, after the adventure with Lavelotte's widow. He made his parent work hard at the boat, and in winter walked him to and from mass literally with hand on collar. He encouraged the little man, moreover, with a half interest in their house on the beach, which long-accumulated earnings of the boat paid for. But all this care was thrown away; though after Jules brought Therese home, and saw that Honoré was not appeased by a woman's cooking, he had qualms about the homestead, and secretly carried the deed back to the original owner.

"I want you keep my part of de deed," he explained. "I not let some more women rob Honoré. My wife, if she get de deed in her han', she might sell de whole t'ing!"

"Why, no, Jules, she couldn't sell your real estate!" the former owner declared. "She would only have a life interest in your share."

"You say she couldn't sell it?"

"No. She would have nothing but a life interest."

"She have only life interest? By gar! I t'ink I pay somebody twenty dollar to kill her!"

But lacking both twenty dollars and determina-

THE MOTHERS OF HONORÉ

tion, he lived peaceably with Therese until she died a natural death, on that occasion proudly doing his whole duty as a man and a mourner.

Remembering these affairs, which had not been kept secret from anybody on the island, Clethera spoke out under conviction.

"Honoré, it a scandal' t'ing, to get marry."

"Me, I t'ink so too," assented Honoré.

"Jules McCarty have disgrace' his son!"

"Melinda Cree," retorted Honoré, obliged to defend his own, "she take a little 'usban' honly nineteen."

"She 'ave no chance like Jules; she is oblige' to wait and take what invite her."

The voices of children from other quarter-breed cottages, playing along the beach, added cheer to the sweet darkness. Clethera and Honoré sat silently enjoying each other's company, unconscious that their aboriginal forefathers had courted in that manner, sitting under arbors of branches.

"Why do peop' want to get marry?" propounded Clethera.

"I don't know," said Honoré.

"Me, if some man hask me, I box his ear! I have know you all my life — but don' you never hask me to get marry!"

"I not such a fool," heartily responded Honoré. "You and me, we have seen de folly. I not form de habit, like Jules."

"But what we do, Honoré, to keep dat Jules and dat Melinda apart?"

Though they discussed many plans, the sequel showed that nothing effectual could be done. All their traditions and instincts were against making themselves disagreeable or showing discourtesy to their elders. The young man's French and Irish and Chippewa blood, and the young girl's French and Cree blood exhausted all their inherited diplomacy. But as steadily as the waters set like a strong tide through the strait, in spite of wind which combed them to ridging foam, the rapid courtship of age went on.

In carrying laundered clothing through the village street, Melinda Cree was carefully chaperoned by her granddaughter, and Honoré kept Jules under orders in the boat. But of early mornings and late twilights there was no restraining the twittering widower.

"Melinda 'tend to her work and is behave if Jules let her alone," Clethera reported to Honoré. "But he slip around de garden and talk over de back fence, and he is by de ironing-board de minute my back is turn'! If he belong to me, I could 'mos' whip him!"

"Jules McCarty," declared Honoré, with some bitterness, "when he fix his min' to marry some more, he is not turn' if he is hexcommunicate'!"

Jules, indeed, became so bold that he crowded across the stile through the very conferences of the pair united to prevent him; and his loud voice could be heard beside Melinda's ironing-board, proclaiming in the manner of a callow young suitor.

"Some peop' like separate us, Melinda, but we not let them."

The conflict of Honoré and Clethera with Jules and Melinda ended one day in August. There had been no domestic clamor in this silent grapple of forces. The young man used no argument except maxims and morals and a tightening of authority; the young girl permitted neither neighboring maids nor the duties of religion to lure her off guard. It may be said of any French half-breed that he has all the instincts of gentility except an inclination to lying, and that arises from excessive politeness.

Honoré came to the fence at noon and called Clethera. In his excitement he crossed the stile and stood on her premises.

"It no use, Clethera. Jules have tell me this morning he have arrange' de marriage."

Clethera glanced behind her at the house she called home, and threw herself in Honoré's arms, as she had often done in childish despairs. Neither misunderstood the action, and it relieved them to shed a few tears on each other's necks. This truly Latin outburst being over, they stood apart and wiped their eyes on their sleeves.

"It no use," exclaimed Clethera, "to set a good examp' to your grandmother!"

"I not wait any longer now," announced Honoré, giving rein to fierce eagerness. "I go to de war to-day."

"But de camp is move'," objected Clethera.

"I have pass' de examin', and I know de man to

go to when I am ready ; he promis' to get me into
de war. Jules have de sails up now, ready to take
me across to de train."

" But who will have de boat when you are gone,
Honoré?"

" Jules. And he bring Melinda to de house."

" She not come. She not leave her own house.
She take her 'usban' in."

" Then Jules must rent de house. You not detest poor Jules ?"

" I not detest him like de hudder one."

" Au 'voir, Clethera."

" Au 'voir, Honoré."

They shook hands, the young man wringing himself away with the animation of one who goes, the
girl standing in the dull anxiety of one who stays.
War, so remote that she had heard of it indiffer-
ently, rushed suddenly from the tropics over the
island.

" Are your clothes all mend' and ready, Honoré ?"

But what thought can a young man give to his
clothes when about to wrap himself in glory ? He
is politely tapping at the shed window of the Indian woman, and touching his cap in farewell and
gallant capitulation, and with long-limbed sweeping
haste, unusual in a quarter-breed, he is gone to the
docks, with a bundle under one arm, waving his
hand as he passes. All the women and children
along the street would turn out to see him go to
the war if his intention were known, and even sum-

mer idlers about the bazars would look at him with new interest.

Clethera could not imagine the moist and horrid heat of those southern latitudes into which Honoré departed to throw himself. Shifting mists on the lake rim were no vaguer than her conception of her country's mighty undertaking. But she could feel; and the life she had lived to that day was wrenched up by the roots, leaving her as with a bleeding socket.

All afternoon she drenched herself with soapsuds in the ferocity of her washing. By the time Jules returned with the boat, the lake was black as ink under a storm cloud, with glints of steel; a dull bar stretched diagonally across the water. Beyond that a whitening of rain showed against the horizon. Points of cedars on the opposite island pricked a sullen sky.

Clethera's tubs were under the trees. She paid no attention to what befell her, or to her grandmother, who called her out of the rain. It came like a powder of dust, and then a moving, blanched wall, pushing islands of flattened mist before it. Under a steady pour the waters turned dull green, and lightened shade by shade as if diluting an infusion of grass. Waves began to come in regular windrows. Though Clethera told herself savagely she not care for anything in de world, her Indian eye took joy of these sights. The shower-bath from the trees she endured without a shiver.

Jules sat beside Melinda to be comforted. He

wept for Honoré, and praised his boy, gasconading with time-worn boasts.

"I got de hang of him, and now I got to part! But de war will end, now Honoré have gone into it. His gran'fodder was such a fighter when de British come to take de island, he turn' de cannon and blow de British off. The gran'fodder of Honoré was a fine man. He always keep de bes' liquors and hy wines on his sideboa'd."

When Honoré had been gone twenty-four hours, and Jules was still idling like a boy undriven by his task-master, leaving the boat to rock under bare poles at anchor on the rise and fall of the water, Clethera went into their empty house. It contained three rooms, and she laid violent hands on male housekeeping. The service was almost religious, like preparing linen for an altar. It comforted her unacknowledged anguish, which increased rather than diminished, the unrest of which she resented with all her stoic Indian nature.

Nets, sledge-harness, and Honoré's every-day clothes hung on his whitewashed wall. The most touching relic of any man is the hat he has worn. Honoré's cap crowned the post of his bed like a wraith. The room might have been a young hermit's cell in a cave, or a tunnel in the evergreens, it was so simple and bare of human appointments. Clethera stood with the broom in one hand, and tipped forward a piece of broken looking-glass on his shaving-shelf. A new, unforeseen Clethera, whom she had never been obliged to deal with before, gave her a desperate, stony stare out of a haggard face. She was young, her skin had not a line. But it was as if she had changed places with her wrinkled grandmother, to whom the expression of complacent maidenhood now belonged.

As Clethera propped the glass again in place, she heard Jules come in. She resumed her sweeping with resolute strokes on the bare boards, which would explain to his ear the necessity of her presence. He appeared at the door, and it was Honoré!

It was Honoré, shamefaced but laughing, back from the war within twenty-four hours! Clethera heard the broom-handle strike the floor as one hears the far-off fall of a spar on a ship in harbor. She put her palms together, without flying into his arms or even offering to shake hands.

"You come back?" she cried out, her voice sharpened by joy.

"The war is end'," said Honoré. "Peace is declare' yesterday!" He threw his bundle down and looked fondly around the rough walls. "All de peop' laugh at me because I go to war when de war is end'!"

"They laugh because de war is end'! I laugh too?" said Clethera, relaxing to sobs. Tears and cries which had been shut up a day and a night were let loose with French abandon. Honoré opened his arms to comfort her in the old manner, and although she rushed into them, strange embarrassment went with her. The two could not look at each other.

"It is de 'omesick," she explained. "When you go to war it make me 'omesick."

"Me, too," owned Honoré. "I never know what it is before. I not mind de fighting, but I am glad de war is end', account of de 'omesick!"

He pushed the hair from her wet face. The fate of temperament and the deep tides of existence had them in merciless sweep.

"Clethera," represented Honoré, "the rillation is not mix' bad with Jules and Melinda."

Clethera let the assertion pass unchallenged.

"And this house, it pretty good house. You like it well as de hudder?"

"It have no loft," responded Clethera, faintly, "but de chimney not smoke."

"We not want de 'omesick some more, Clethera—eh? You t'ink de fools is all marry yet?"

Clethera laughed and raised her head from his arm, but not to look at him or box his ear. She looked through the open door at an oblong of little world, where the land was an amethyst strip betwixt lake and horizon. Across that beloved background she saw the future pass: hale, long years with Honoré; the piled up wood of winter fires; her own home; her children—the whole scheme of sweet and humble living.

"You t'ink, after all de folly we have see' in de family, Clethera, you can go de lenk — to get marry?"

"I go dat lenk for you, Honoré—but not for any hudder man."

"HE APPEARED AT THE DOOR, AND IT WAS HONORÉ"

THE BLUE MAN

THE lake was like a meadow full of running streams. Far off indeed it seemed frozen, with countless wind-paths traversing the ice, so level and motionless was the surface under a gray sky. But summer rioted in verdure over the cliffs to the very beaches. From the high greenery of the island could be heard the tink-tank of a bell where some cow sighed amid the delicious gloom.

East of the Giant's Stairway in a cove are two round rocks with young cedars springing from them. It is easy to scramble to the flat top of the first one and sit in open ambush undetected by passers. The world's majority is unobservant. Children with their nurses, lovers, bicyclists who have left their wheels behind, excursionists — fortunately headed towards this spot in their one available hour—an endless procession, tramp by on the rough, wave-lapped margin, never wearing it smooth.

Amused by the unconsciousness of the reviewed, I found myself unexpectedly classed with the world's majority. For on the east round rock, a few yards from my seat on the west round rock, behold a man had arranged himself, his back against the cedars, without attracting notice. While the gray weather lightened and wine-red streaks on the lake began to alternate with translucent greens, and I was watching mauve plumes spring from a distant steamer before her whistles could be heard, this nimble stranger must have found his own amusement in the blindness of people with eyes.

He was not quite a stranger. I had seen him the day before; and he was a man to be remembered on account of a peculiar blueness of the skin, in which, perhaps, some drug or chemical had left an unearthly haze over the natural flush of blood. It might have appeared the effect of sky lights and cliff shadows, if I had not seen the same blue face distinctly in Madame Clementine's house. He was standing in the middle of a room at the foot of the stairway as we passed his open door.

So unusual a personality was not out of place in a transplanted Parisian tenement. Madame Clementine was a Parisian; and her house, set around three sides of a quadrangle in which flowers overflowed their beds, was a bit of artisan Paris. The ground-floor consisted of various levels joined by steps and wide-jambed doors. The chambers, to which a box staircase led, wanted nothing except canopies over the beds.

" Alors I give de convenable beds," said Madame Clementine, in mixed French and English, as she poked her mattresses. " Des bons lits! T'ree dollar one chambre, four dollar one chambre—" she suddenly spread her hands to include both—" seven dollar de tout ensemble!"

It was delightful to go with any friend who might be forced by crowded hotels to seek rooms in Madame Clementine's alley. The active, tiny Frenchwoman, who wore a black mob-cap everywhere except to mass, had reached present prosperity through past tribulation. Many years before she had followed a runaway husband across the sea. As she stepped upon the dock almost destitute the first person her eyes rested on was her husband standing well forward in the crowd, with a ham under his arm which he was carrying home to his family. He saw Clementine and dropped the ham to run. The same hour he took his new wife and disappeared from the island. The doubly deserted French-speaking woman found employment and friends; and by her thrift was now in the way of piling up what she considered a fortune.

The man on the rock near me was no doubt one of Madame Clementine's permanent lodgers. Tourists ranting over the island in a single day had not his repose. He met my discovering start with a dim smile and a bend of his head, which was bare. His features were large, and his mouth corners had the sweet, strong expression of a noble patience. What first impressed me seemed to be his blueness, and the blurredness of his eyes struggling to sight as Bartimeus' eyes might have struggled the instant before the Lord touched them.

Only Asiatics realize the power of odors. The

sense of smell is lightly appreciated in the Western
world. A fragrance might be compounded which
would have absolute power over a human being.
We get wafts of scent to which something in us irresistibly answers. A satisfying sweetness, fleeting
as last year's wild flowers, filled the whole cove.
I thought of dead Indian pipes, standing erect in
pathetic dignity, the delicate scales on their stems
unfurled, refusing to crumble and pass away; the
ghosts of Indians.

The blue man parted his large lips and moved
them several instants; then his voice followed, like
the tardy note of a distant steamer that addresses
the eye with its plume of steam before the whistle
is heard. I felt a creepy thrill down my shoulders
—that sound should break so slowly across the few
yards separating us! "Are you also waiting, madame?"

I felt compelled to answer him as I would have
answered no other person. "Yes; but for one who
never comes."

If he had spoken in the pure French of the
Touraine country, which is said to be the best in
France, free from Parisianisms, it would not
have surprised me. But he spoke English, with
the halting though clear enunciation of a Nova
Scotian.

"You—you must have patience. I have—have
seen you only seven summers on the island."

"You have seen me these seven years past? But
I never met you before!"

His mouth labored voicelessly before he declared, "I have been here thirty-five years."

How could that be possible!—and never a hint drifting through the hotels of any blue man! Yet the intimate life of old inhabitants is not paraded before the overrunning army of a season. I felt vaguely flattered that this exclusive resident had hitherto noticed me and condescended at last to reveal himself.

The blue man had been here thirty-five years! He knew the childish joy of bruising the flesh of orange-colored toadstools and wading amid long pine-cones which strew the ground like fairy corn-cobs. The white birches were dear to him, and he trembled with eagerness at the first pipe sign, or at the discovery of blue gentians where the eastern forest stoops to the strand. And he knew the echo, shaking like gigantic organ music from one side of the world to the other.

In solitary trysts with wilderness depths and caves which transient sight-seers know nothing about I had often pleased myself thinking the Mishi-ne-macki-naw-go were somewhere around me. If twigs crackled or a sudden awe fell causelessly, I laughed—"That family of Indian ghosts is near. I wish they would show themselves!" For if they ever show themselves, they bring you the gift of prophecy. The Chippewas left tobacco and gunpowder about for them. My offering was to cover with moss the picnic papers, tins, and broken bottles, with which man who is vile defiles every prospect. Discovering such a queer islander as the blue man was almost equal to seeing the Mishi-ne-macki-naw-go.

Voices approached; and I watched his eyes come into his face as he leaned forward! From a blurr of lids they turned to beautiful clear balls shot through with yearning. Around the jut of rock appeared a bicycle girl, a golf girl, and a youth in knickers having his stockings laid in correct folds below the knee. They passed without noticing us. To see his looks dim and his eagerness relax was too painful. I watched the water ridging against the horizon like goldstone and changing swiftly to the blackest of greens. Distance folded into distance so that the remote drew near. He was certainly waiting for somebody, but it could not be that he had waited thirty-five years: thirty-five winters, whitening the ice-bound island; thirty-five summers, bringing all paradise except what he waited for.

Just as I glanced at the blue man again his lips began to move, and the peculiar tingle ran down my back, though I felt ashamed of it in his sweet presence.

"Madame, it will—it will comfort me if you permit me to talk to you."

"I shall be very glad, sir, to hear whatever you have to tell."

"I have—have waited here thirty-five years, and in all that time I have not spoken to any one!"

He said this quite candidly, closing his lips before

his voice ceased to sound. The cedar sapling against which his head rested was not more real than the sincerity of that blue man's face. Some hermit soul, who had proved me by watching me seven years, was opening himself, and I felt the tears come in my eyes.

"Have you never heard of me, madame?"

"You forget, sir, that I do not even know your name."

"My name is probably forgotten on the island now. I stopped here between steamers during your American Civil War. A passing boat put in to leave a young girl who had cholera. I saw her hair floating out of the litter."

"Oh!" I exclaimed; "that is an island story." The blue man was actually presenting credentials when he spoke of the cholera story. "She was taken care of on the island until she recovered; and she was the beautiful daughter of a wealthy Southern family trying to get home from her convent in France, but unable to run the blockade. The nun who brought her died on shipboard before she landed at Montreal, and she hoped to get through the lines by venturing down the lakes. Yes, indeed! Madame Clementine has told me that story."

He listened, turning his head attentively and keeping his eyes half closed, and again worked his lips.

"Yes, yes. You know where she was taken care of?"

"It was at Madame Clementine's."

"I myself took her there."

"And have you been there ever since?"

He passed over the trivial question, and when his voice arrived it gushed without a stammer.

"I had a month of happiness. I have had thirty-five years of waiting. When this island binds you to any one you remain bound. Since that month with her I can do nothing but wait until she comes. I lost her, I don't know how. We were in this cove together. She sat on this rock and waited while I went up the cliff to gather ferns for her. When I returned she was gone. I searched the island for her. It kept on smiling as if there never had been such a person! Something happened which I do not understand, for she did not want to leave me. She disappeared as if the earth had swallowed her!"

I felt a rill of cold down my back like the jetting of the spring that spouted from its ferny tunnel farther eastward. Had he been thirty-five years on the island without ever hearing the Old Mission story about bones found in the cliff above us? Those who reached them by venturing down a pit as deep as a well, uncovered by winter storms, declared they were the remains of a woman's skeleton. I never saw the people who found them. It was an oft-repeated Mission story which had come down to me. An Indian girl was missed from the Mission school and never traced. It was believed she met her fate in this rock crevasse. The bones were blue, tinged by a clay in which they had lain. I tried to remember what became of the Southern girl who was put ashore, her hair flying from a litter. Distinct as her tradition remained, it ended abruptly. Even Madame Clementine forgot when and how she left the island after she ceased to be an object of solicitude, for many comers and goers trample the memory as well as the island.

Had his love followed him up the green tangled height and sunk so swiftly to her death that it was accomplished without noise or outcry? To this hour only a few inhabitants locate the treacherous spot. He could not hide, even at Madame Clementine's, from all the talk of a community. This unreasonable tryst of thirty-five years raised for the first time doubts of his sanity. A woman might have kept such a tryst; but a man consoles himself.

Passers had been less frequent than usual, but again there was a crunch of approaching feet. Again he leaned forward, and the sparks in his eyes enlarged, and faded, as two fat women wobbled over the unsteady stones, exclaiming and balancing themselves, oblivious to the blue man and me.

"It is four o'clock," said one, pausing to look at her watch. "This air gives one such an appetite I shall never be able to wait for dinner."

"When the girls come in from golf at five we will have some tea," said the other.

Returning beach gadders passed us. Some of them noticed me with a start, but the blue man, wrapped in rigid privacy, with his head sunk on his breast, still evaded curious eyes.

I began to see that his clothes were by no means new, though they suited the wearer with a kind of masculine elegance. The blue man's head had so entirely dominated my attention that the cut of his coat and his pointed collar and neckerchief seemed to appear for the first time.

He turned his face to me once more, but before our brief talk could be resumed another woman came around the jut of cliff, so light-footed that she did not make as much noise on the stones as the fat women could still be heard making while they floundered eastward, their backs towards us. The blue man had impressed me as being of middle age. But I felt mistaken; he changed so completely. Springing from the rock like a boy, his eyes glorified, his lips quivering, he met with open arms the woman who had come around the jut of the Giant's Stairway. At first glance I thought her a slim old woman with the kind of hair which looks either blond or gray. But the maturity glided into sinuous girlishness, yielding to her lover, and her hair shook loose, floating over his shoulder.

I dropped my eyes. I heard a pebble stir under their feet. The tinkle of water falling down its ferny tunnel could be guessed at; and the beauty of the world stabbed one with such keenness that the stab brought tears.

We have all had our dreams of flying; or floating high or low, lying extended on the air at will. By what process of association I do not know, the perfect naturalness and satisfaction of flying recurred to me. I was cleansed from all doubt of ultimate good. The meeting of the blue man and the woman with floating hair seemed to be what the island had awaited for thirty-five years.

The miracle of impossible happiness had been worked for him. It confused me like a dazzle of fireworks. I turned my back and bowed my head, waiting for him to speak again or to leave me out, as he saw fit.

Extreme joy may be very silent in those who have waited long, for I did not hear a cry or a spoken word. Presently I dared to look, and was not surprised to find myself alone. The evergreen-clothed amphitheatre behind had many paths which would instantly hide climbers from view. The blue man and the woman with floating hair knew these heights well. I thought of the pitfall, and sat watching with back-tilted head, anxious to warn them if they stirred foliage near where that fatal trap was said to lurk. But the steep forest gave no sign or sound from its mossy depths.

I sat still a long time in a trance of the senses, like that which follows a drama whose spell you would not break. Masts and cross-trees of ships were banded by ribbons of smoke blowing back from the steamers which towed them in lines up or down the straits.

Towards sunset there was a faint blush above the steel-blue waters, which at their edge reflected the blush. Then mist closed in. The sky became ribbed with horizontal bars, so that the earth was

197

pent like a heart within the hollow of some vast skeleton.

I was about to climb down from my rock when two young men passed by, the first strollers I had noticed since the blue man's exit. They rapped stones out of the way with their canes, and pushed the caps back from their youthful faces, talking rapidly in excitement.

"When did it happen?"

"About four o'clock. You were off at the golf links."

"Was she killed instantly?"

"I think so. I think she never knew what hurt her after seeing the horses plunge and the carriage go over. I was walking my wheel down-hill just behind and I didn't hear her scream. The driver said he lost the brake; and he's a pretty spectacle now, for he landed on his head. It was that beautiful old lady with the fly-away hair that we saw arrive from this morning's boat while we were sitting out smoking, you remember."

"Not that one!"

"That was the woman. Had a black maid with her. She's a Southerner. I looked on the register."

The other young fellow whistled.

"I'm glad I was at the links and didn't see it. She was a stunning woman."

Dusk stalked grimly down from eastern heights and blurred the water earlier than on rose-colored evenings, making the home-returning walker shiver through evergreen glooms along shore. The lights of the sleepy Old Mission had never seemed so pleasant, though the house was full of talk about that day's accident at the other side of the island.

I slipped out before the early boat left next morning, driven by undefined anxieties towards Madame Clementine's alley. There is a childish credulity which clings to imaginative people through life. I had accepted the blue man and the woman with floating hair in the way which they chose to present themselves. But I began to feel like one who sees a distinctly focused picture shimmering to a dissolving view. The intrusion of an accident to a stranger at another hotel continued this morning, for as I took the long way around the bay before turning back to Clementine's alley I met the open island hearse, looking like a relic of provincial France, and in it was a coffin, and behind it moved a carriage in which a black maid sat weeping.

Madame Clementine came out to her palings and picked some of her nasturtiums for me. In her mixed language she talked excitedly about the accident; nothing equals the islander's zest for sensation after his winter trance when the summer world comes to him.

"When I heard it," I confessed, "I thought of the friend of your blue gentleman. The description was so like her. But I saw her myself on the beach by the Giant's Stairway after four o'clock yesterday."

Madame Clementine contracted her short face in puzzled wrinkles.

"There is one gentleman of red head," she responded, "but none of blue—pas du tout."

"You must know whom I mean—the lodger who has been with you thirty-five years."

She looked at me as at one who has either been tricked or is attempting trickery.

"I don't know his name—but you certainly understand! The man I saw in that room at the foot of the stairs when you were showing my friend and me the chambers day before yesterday."

"There was nobody. De room at de foot of de stair is empty all season. Tout de suite I put in some young lady that arrive this night."

"Madame Clementine, I saw a man with a blue skin on the beach yesterday—" I stopped. He had not told me he lodged with her. That was my own deduction. "I saw him the day before in this house. Don't you know any such person? He has been on the island since that young lady was brought to your house with the cholera so long ago. He brought her to you."

A flicker of recollection appeared on Clementine's face.

"That man is gone, madame; it is many years. And he was not blue at all. He was English Jersey man, of Halifax."

"Did you never hear of any blue man on the island, Clementine?"

"I hear of blue bones found beyond Point de Mission."

" But that skeleton found in the hole near the Giant's Stairway was a woman's skeleton."

" Me loes!" exclaimed Madame Clementine, miscalling her English as she always did in excitement. " Me handle de big bones, moi-même! Me loes what de doctor who found him say!"

" I was told it was an Indian girl."

" You have hear lies, madame. Me loes there was a blue man found beyond Point de Mission."

" But who was it that I saw in your house?"

" He is not in my house!" declared Madame Clementine. " No blue man is ever in my house!" She crossed herself.

There is a sensation like having a slide pulled from one's head; the shock passes in the fraction of a second. Sunshine, and rioting nasturtiums, the whole natural world, including Clementine's puzzled brown face, were no more distinct to-day than the blue man and the woman with floating hair had been yesterday.

I had seen a man who shot down to instant death in the pit under the Giant's Stairway thirty-five years ago. I had seen a woman, who, perhaps, once thought herself intentionally and strangely deserted, seek and meet him after she had been killed at four o'clock!

This experience, set down in my note-book and repeated to no one, remains associated with the Old World scent of ginger. For I remember hearing Clementine say through a buzzing, " You come in, madame—you must have de hot wine and jahjah!"

201

THE INDIAN ON THE TRAIL

MAURICE BARRETT sat waiting in the old lime-kiln built by the British in the war of 1812—a white ruin like much-scattered marble, which stands bowered in trees on a high part of the island. He had, to the amusement of the commissioner, hired this place for a summer study, and paid a carpenter to put a temporary roof over it, with skylight, and to make a door which could be fastened. Here on the uneven floor of stone were set his desk, his chair, and a bench on which he could stretch himself to think when undertaking to make up arrears in literary work. But the days were becoming nothing but trysts with her for whom he waited.

First came the heavenly morning walk and the opening of his study, then the short half-hour of labor, which ravelled off to delicious suspense. He caught through trees the hint of a shirt-waist which might be any girl's, then the long exquisite outline which could be nobody's in the world but hers, her face under its sailor hat, the blown blond hair, the blue eyes. Then her little hands met his out-stretched hands at the door, and her whole violet-breathing self yielded to his arms.

They sat down on the bench, still in awe of each other and of the swift miracle of their love and engagement. Maurice had passed his fiftieth year, so clean from dissipation, so full of vitality and the beauty of a long race of strong men, that he did not look forty, and in all out-door activities rivalled the boys in their early twenties. He was an expert mountain-climber and explorer of regions from which he brought his own literary material; inured to fatigue, patient in hardship, and resourceful in danger. Money and reputation and the power which attends them he had wrung from fate as his right, and felt himself fit to match with the best blood in the world—except hers.

Yet she was only his social equal, and had grown up next door, while his unsatisfied nature searched the universe for its mate—a wild sweetbrier-rose of a child, pink and golden, breathing a daring, fragrant personality. He hearkened back to some recognition of her charm from the day she ran out bareheaded and slim-legged on her father's lawn and turned on the hose for her play. Yet he barely missed her when she went to an Eastern school, and only thrilled vaguely when she came back like one of Gibson's pictures, carrying herself with stateliness. There was something in her blue eyes not to be found in any other blue eyes. He was housed with her family in the same hotel at the island before he completely understood the magnitude of what had befallen him.

"I am awfully set up because you have chosen me," she admitted at first. He liked to have her proud as of a conquest, and he was conscious of that general favor which stamped him a good match, even for a girl half his age.

"How much have you done this morning?" she inquired, looking at his desk.

"Enough to tide over the time until you came. Determination and execution are not one with me now." Her hands were cold, and he warmed them against his face.

"It was during your married life that determination and execution were one?"

"Decidedly. For that was my plodding age. Sometimes when I am tingling with impatience here I look back in wonder on the dogged drive of those days. Work is an unhappy man's best friend. I have no concealments from you, Lily. You know I never loved my wife—not this way—though I made her happy; I did my duty. She told me when she died that I had made her happy. People cannot help their limitations."

"Do you love me?" she asked, her lips close to his ear.

"I am you! Your blood flows through my veins. I feel you rush through me. You don't know what it is to love like that, do you?"

She shook her head.

"When you are out of my sight I do not live; I

simply wait. What is the weird power in you that creates such gigantic passion?"

"The power is all in your imagination. You simply don't know me. You think I am a prize. Why, I—flirt—and I've—kissed men!"

He laughed. "You would be a queer girl, at your age, if you hadn't — kissed men — a little. Whatever your terrible past has been, it has made you the infinite darling that you are!"

She moved her eyes to watch the leaves twinkling in front of the lime-kiln.

"I must go," she said.

"'I must go'!" he mocked. "You are no sooner here than—'I must go'!"

"I can't be with you all the time. You don't care for appearances, so I have to."

"Appearances are nothing. This is the only real thing in the universe."

"But I really must go." She lifted her wilful chin and sat still. They stared at each other in the silence of lovers. Though the girl's face was without a line, she was more skilled in the play of love than he.

"Indeed I must go. Your eyes are half shut, like a gentian."

"When you are living intensely you don't look at the world through wide-open eyes," said Maurice. "I never let myself go before. Repression has been the law of my life. Think of it! In a long life-time I have loved but two persons—the woman I told you of, and you. Twenty years ago

I found out what life meant. For the first time, I knew! But I was already married. I took that beautiful love by the throat and choked it down. Afterwards, when I was free, the woman I first loved was married. How long I have had to wait for you to bloom, lotos flower! This is living! All the other years were preparation."

"Do you never see her?" inquired the girl.

"Who? That first one? I have avoided her."

"She loved you?"

"With the blameless passion that we both at first thought was the most perfect friendship."

"Wouldn't you marry her now if she were free?"

"No. It is ended. We have grown apart in renunciation for twenty years. I am not one that changes easily, you see. You have taken what I could not withhold from you, and it is yours. I am in your power."

They heard a great steamer blowing upon the strait. Its voice reverberated through the woods. The girl's beautiful face was full of a tender wistfulness, half maternal. Neither jealousy nor pique marred its exquisite sympathy. It was such an expression as an untamed wood-nymph might have worn, contemplating the life of man.

"Don't be sad," she breathed.

Vague terror shot through Maurice's gaze.

"That is a strange thing for you to say to me, Lily. Is it all you can say—when I love you so?"

"I was thinking of the other woman. Did she suffer?"

"At any rate, she has the whole world now—beauty, talent, wealth, social prestige. She is one of the most successful women in this country."

"Do I know her name?"

"Quite well. She has been a person of consequence since you were a child."

"I couldn't capture the whole world," mused Lily. Maurice kissed her small fingers.

"Some one else will put it in your lap, to keep or throw away as you choose."

The hurried tink-tank of an approaching cow-bell suggested passers. Then a whir of wheels could be heard through tangled wilderness. The girl met his lips with a lingering which trembled through all his body, and withdrew herself.

"Now I am going. Are you coming down the trail with me?"

Maurice shut the lime-kiln door, and crossed with her a grassy avenue to find among birches the ravelled ends of a path called the White Islander's Trail. You may know it first by a triangle of roots at the foot of an oak. Thence a thread, barely visible to expert eyes, winds to some mossy dead pines and crosses a rotten log. There it becomes a trail cleaving the heights, and plunging boldly up and down evergreen glooms to a road parallel with the cliff. Once, when the island was freshly drenched in rain, Lily breathed deeply, gazing down the tunnel floored with rock and pine-needles, a flask of incense. "It is like the violins!"

In that seclusion of heaven Maurice could draw

her slim shape to him, for the way is so narrow that two are obliged to walk close. They parted near the wider entrance, where a stump reared itself against the open sky, bearing a stick like a bow, and having the appearance of a crouching figure.

"There is the Indian on the trail," said Lily. "You must go back now."

"He looks so formidable," said Maurice; "especially in twilight, and, except at noon, it is always twilight here. But when you reach him he is nothing but a stump."

"He is more than a stump," she insisted. "He is a real Indian, and some day will get up and take a scalp! It gives me a shiver every time I come in sight of him crouched on the trail!"

"Do you know," complained her lover, "that you haven't told me once to-day?"

"Well—I do."

"How much?"

"Oh—a little!"

"A little will not do!"

"Then—a great deal."

"I want all—all!"

Her eyes wandered towards the Indian on the trail, and the bow of her mouth was bent in a tantalizing curve.

"I have told you I love you. Why doesn't that satisfy you?"

"It isn't enough!"

"Perhaps I can't satisfy you. I love you all I can."

"All you can?"

"Yes. Maybe I can't love you as much as you want me to. I am shallow!"

"For God's sake, don't say you are shallow! There is deep under deep in you! I couldn't have staked my life on you, I couldn't have loved you, if there hadn't been! Say I have only touched the surface yet, but don't say you are shallow!"

The girl shook her head.

"There isn't enough of me. Do you know," she exclaimed, whimsically, "that's the Indian on the trail! You'll never feel quite sure of me, will you?"

Maurice's lips moved. "You are my own!"

She kept him at bay with her eyes, though they filled slowly with tears.

"I am a child of the devil!" exclaimed Lily, with vehemence. "I give people trouble and make them suffer!"

"She classes me with 'people'!" Maurice thought. He said, "Have I ever blamed you for anything?"

"No."

"Then don't blame yourself. I will simply take what you can give me. That is all I could take. Forgive me for loving you too much. I will try to love you less."

"No," the girl demurred. "I don't want you to do that."

"I am very unreasonable," he said, humbly. "But the rest of the world is a shadow. You are my one reality. There is nothing in the universe but you."

She brushed her eyes fiercely. "I mustn't cry. I'll have to explain it if I do, and the lids will be red all day."

The man felt internally seared, as by burning lava, with the conviction that he had staked his all late in life on what could never be really his. She would diffuse herself through many. He was concentrated in her. His passion had its lips burned shut.

"I am Providence's favorite bag-holder," was his bitter thought. "The game is never for me."

"Good-bye," said Lily.

"Good-bye," said Maurice.

"Are you coming into the casino to-night?"

"If you will be there."

"I have promised a lot of dances. Good-bye. Go back and work."

"Yes, I must work," said Maurice.

She gave him a defiant, radiant smile, and ran towards the Indian on the trail. He turned in the opposite direction, and tramped the woods until nightfall.

At first he mocked himself. "Oh yes, she loves me! I'm glad, at any rate, that she loves me! There will be enough to moisten my lips with; and if I thirst for an ocean that is not her fault."

Why had a woman been made who could inspire such passion without returning it? He reminded himself that she was of a later, a gayer, lighter, less strenuous generation than his own. Thousands of men had waded blood for a principle and a lost cause in his day. In hers the gigantic republic stood up a menace to nations. The struggle for existence was over before she was born. Yet women seemed more in earnest now than ever before. He said to himself, "I have always picked out natures as fatal to me as a death-warrant, and fastened my life to them."

The thought stabbed him that perhaps his wife, whom he had believed satisfied, had carried such hopeless anguish as he now carried. Tardy remorse for what he could not help gave him the feeling of a murderer. And since he knew himself how little may be given under the bond of marriage, he could not look forward and say, "My love will yet be mine!"

He would, indeed, have society on his side; and children—he drew his breath hard at that. Her ways with children were divine. He had often watched her instinctive mothering of, and drawing them around her. And it should be much to him that he might look at and touch her. There was life in her mere presence.

He felt the curse of the artistic temperament, which creates in man the exquisite sensitiveness of woman.

Taking the longest and hardest path home around the eastern beach, Maurice turned once on impulse, parted a screen of birches, and stepped into an amphitheatre of the cliff, moss-clothed and cedar-walled. It sloped downward in three terraces. A balcony or high parapet of stone hung on one side, a rock low and broad stood in the centre, and an unmistakable chair of rock, cushioned with vividly green-branched moss, waited an occupant. Maurice sat down, wondering if any other human being, perplexed and tortured, had ever domiciled there for a brief time. Slim alder-trees and maples were clasped in moss to their waists. The spacious open was darkened by dense shade overhead. Bois Blanc was plainly in view from the beach. But the eastern islands stretched a line of foliage in growing dusk. Maurice felt the cooling benediction of the place. This world is such a good world to be happy in, if you have the happiness.

When the light faded he went on, climbing low headlands which jutted into the water, and sliding down on the other side; so that he reached the hotel physically exhausted, and had his dinner sent to his room. But a vitality constantly renewing itself swept away every trace of his hard day when he entered the gayly lighted casino.

He no longer danced, not because dancing ceased to delight him, but because the serious business of life had left no room for it. He walked along the waxed floor, avoiding the circling procession of waltzers, and bowing to a bank of pretty faces, but thinking his own thought, in growing bitterness: "They who live blameless lives are the fools of fate. If I had it to do over again, I would take what I wanted in spite of everything, and let the consequences fall where they would!" Looking up, he met in the eyes the woman of his early love.

She was holding court, for a person of such consequence became the centre of the caravansary from the instant of her arrival; and she gave him her hand with the conventional frankness and self-command that set her apart from the weak. Once more he knew she was a woman to be worshipped, whose presence rebuked the baseness he had just thought.

"Perhaps it was she who kept me from being worse," Maurice recognized in a flash; "not I myself!"

"Why, Mrs. Carstang, I didn't know you were here!" he spoke, with warmth around the heart.

"We came at noon."

"And I was in the woods all day." Maurice greeted the red-cheeked, elderly Mr. Carstang, whom, according to half the world, his wife doted upon, and according to the other half, she simply endured. At any rate, he looked pleased with his lot.

While Maurice stood talking with Mrs. Carstang, the new grief and the old strangely neutralized each other. It was as if they met and grappled, and he had numb peace. The woman of his first love made him proud of that early bond. She was more than she had been then. But Lily moved past him with a smile. Her dancing was visible music. It had a penetrating grace—hers, and no other person's in the world. The floating of a slim nymph down a forest avenue, now separating from her partner, and now joining him at caprice, it rushed through Maurice like some recollection of the Golden Age, when he had stood imprisoned in a tree. There was little opportunity to do anything but watch her, for she was more in demand than any other girl in the casino. Hop nights were her unconscious ovations. He took a kind of aching delight in her dancing. For while it gratified an artist to the core, it separated her from her lover and gave her to other men.

Next morning he waited for her in the study with a restlessness which would not let him sit still. More than once he went as far as the oak-tree to watch for a glimmer. But when Lily finally appeared at the door he pretended to be very busy with papers on his desk, and looked up, saying, "Oh!"

The morning was chill, and she seemed a fair Russian in fur-edged cloth as she put her cold fingers teasingly against his neck.

"Are you working hard?"

"Trying to. I am behind."

"But if there is a good wind this afternoon you are not to forget the Carstangs' sail. They will be here only a day or two, and you mustn't neglect them. Mrs. Carstang told me if I saw you first to invite you."

Maurice met the girl's smiling eyes, and the ice of her hand went through him.

"Isn't Mrs. Carstang lovely! As soon as I saw you come in last night, I knew she was—the other woman."

"You didn't look at me."

"I can see with my eyelashes. Do you know, I have often thought I should love her if I were a man!"

There was not a trace of jealousy in Lily's gentle and perfect manner.

"You resemble her," said Maurice. "You have the blond head, and the same features—only a little more delicate."

"I have been in her parlor all morning," said Lily. "We talked about you. I am certain, Maurice, Mrs. Carstang is in her heart still faithful to you."

That she should thrust the old love on him as a kind of solace seemed the cruelest of all. There was no cognizance of anything except this one maddening girl. She absorbed him. She wrung the strength of his manhood from him as tribute, such tribute as everybody paid her, even Mrs. Carstang. He sat like a rock, tranced by the strong control which he kept over himself.

"I must go," said Lily. She had not sat down at all. Maurice shuffled his papers.

"Good-bye," she spoke.

"Good-bye," he answered.

She did not ask, "Are you coming down the trail with me?" but ebbed softly away, the swish of her silken petticoat subsiding on the grassy avenue.

Her lover stretched his arms across the desk and sobbed upon them with heart-broken gasps.

"It is killing me! It is killing me! And there is no escape. If I took my life my disembodied ghost would follow her, less able to make itself felt than now! I cannot live without her, and she is not for me—not for me!"

He cursed the necessity which drove him out with the sailing party, and the prodigal waste of life on neutral, trivial doings which cannot be called living. He could see Lily with every pore of his body, and grew faint keeping down a wild beast in him which desired to toss overboard the men who crowded around her. She was more deliciously droll than any comédienne, full of music and wit, the kind of spirit that rises flood-tide with occasion. He was himself hilarious also during this experience of sailing with two queens surrounded by courtiers and playing the deep game of fascination, as if men were created for the amusement of their lighter moments. Lily's defiant, inscrutable eyes mocked him. But Mrs. Carstang gave him sweet friendship, and he sat by her with the unchanging loyalty of a devotee to an altar from which the sacrament has been removed.

Next morning Lily did not come to the lime-kiln. Maurice worked furiously all day, and corrected proof in his room at night, though tableaux were shown in the casino, both Mrs. Carstang and Lily being head and front of the undertaking.

The second day Lily did not come to the lime-kiln. But he saw her pass along the grassy avenue in front of his study with Mrs. Carstang, a man on each side of them. They waved their hands to him.

Maurice sat with his head on his desk all the afternoon, beaten and broken-hearted. He told himself he was a poltroon; that he was losing his manhood; that the one he loved despised him, and did well to despise him; that a man of his age who gave way to such weakness must be entering senility. The habit of rectitude would cover him like armor, and proclaim him still of a chivalry to which he felt recreant. But it came upon him like revelation that many a man had died of what doctors had called disease, when the report to the health-officer should have read: "This man loved a woman with a great passion, and she slew him."

The sigh of the woods around, and the sunlight searching for him through his door, were lonelier than illimitable space. It was what the natives call a "real Mackinac day," with infinite splendor of sky and water.

Maurice heard the rustle of woman's clothes, and stood up as Lily came through the white waste of stones. She stopped and gazed at him with large hunted eyes, and submitted to his taking and kissing her hands. It was so blessed to have her at all that half his trouble fled before her. They sat down together on the bench.

Much of his life Maurice had been in the attitude of judging whether other people pleased him or not. Lily reversed this habit of mind, and made him humbly solicitous to know whether he pleased her or not. He silently thanked God for the mere privilege of having her near him. Passionate selfishness was chastened out of him. One can say much behind the lips and make no sound at all.

"If I drench her with my love and she does not know it," thought Maurice, "it cannot annoy her. Let me take what she is willing to give, and ask no more."

"The Carstangs are gone," said Lily.

"Yes; I bade them good-bye this morning before I came to the lime-kiln."

"You don't say you regret their going."

"I never seek Mrs. Carstang."

He sat holding the girl's hands and never swerving a glance from her face, which was weirdly pallid —the face of her spirit. He felt himself enveloped and possessed by her, his will subject to her will. He said within himself, voicelessly: "I love you. I love the firm chin, the wilful lower lip, and the Cupid's bow of the upper lip. I love the oval of your cheeks, the curve of your ears, the etched eyebrows, and all the little curls on your temples. I love the proud nose and most beautiful forehead. Every blond hair on that dear head is mine! Its upward tilt on the long throat is adorable! Have you any gesture or personal trait which does not thrill me? But best of all, because through them you yourself look at me, revealing more than you think, I adore your blue eyes."

"What are you thinking?" demanded Lily.

"Of a man who lay face downward far out in the desert, and had not a drop of water to moisten his lips."

"Is he in your story?"

"Yes, he is in my story."

"I thought perhaps you didn't want me to come here any more," she said.

"You didn't think so!" flashed Maurice.

"But you turned your cheek to me the last time I was here. You were too busy to do more than speak."

Voicelessly he said : "I lay under your feet, my life, my love! You walked on me and never knew it." Aloud he answered : "Was I so detestable? Forgive me. I am trying to learn self-control."

"You are all self-control! If you have feeling, you manage very well to conceal it."

"God grant it!" he said, in silence, behind his lips. "For the touch of your hand is rapture. My God! how hard it is to love so much and be still!" Aloud he said, "Don't you know the great mass of human beings are obliged to conceal their feelings because they have not the gift of expression?"

"Yes, I know," answered Lily, defiantly.

"But that can never be said of you," Maurice went on. "For you are so richly endowed with expression that your problem is how to mask it."

"Are you coming down the trail with me? It is sunset, and time to shut the study for the day."

He prepared at once to leave his den, and they went out together on the trail, lingering step by step. Though it was the heart of the island summer, the maples still had tender pink leaves at the extremities of branches; and the trail looked wild and fresh as if that hour tunnelled through the wilderness. Sunset tried to penetrate western stretches with level shafts, but none reached the darkening path where twilight already purpled the hollows.

The night coolness was like respite after burning pain. Maurice wondered how close he might draw this changeful girl to him without again losing her. He had compared her to a wild sweetbrier - rose. She was a hundred-leaved rose, hiding innumerable natures in her depths.

They passed the dead pines, crossed the rotten log, and came silently within sight of the Indian on the trail, but neither of them noted it. The Indian stood stencilled against a background of primrose light, his bow magnified.

It was here that Maurice felt the slight elastic body sag upon his arm.

"I am tired," said Lily. "I have been working so hard to amuse your friends!"

"Would that I were my friends!" responded Maurice. He said, silently: "I love you! I wonder if I shall ever learn to love you less?"

The unspoken appeal of her swaying figure put him off his guard, and he found himself holding her, the very depths of his passion rushing out with the force of lava.

"It is you I want!—the you that is not any other person on earth or in the universe! Whatever it is—the identity—the spirit—that is you— the you that was mated with me in other lives—

that I have sought—will seek—must have, whatever the price in time and anguish!—understand!—there is nobody but you!"

Tears oozed from under her closed lids. She lay in his arms passive, as in a half-swoon.

"You do the talking," she breathed. "I do the loving!"

Without opening her eyes she met him with her perfect mouth, and gave herself to him in a kiss. He understood a spirit so passionately reticent that it denied to itself its own inward motions. The wilfulness of a solitary exalted nature melted in that kiss. All the soft curves of her face concealed and belied the woman who opened her wild blue eyes and looked at him, passionately adoring, fierce for her own, yet doubtful of fate.

"If I let you know that I loved you all I do, you would tire of me!"

"How can you say I could ever tire of you?"

"I know it! When you are not quite sure of me, you love me best!"

Maurice laughed against her lips. "You said that was the Indian on the trail—my never being quite sure of you! Will you take an oath with me?"

"Yes."

"This is the oath: I swear before God that I love you more than any one else on earth; more than any one else in the universe."

She repeated: "I swear before God that I love you more than any one else on earth; more than any one else in the universe!"

Maurice held her blond head against his breast, quivering through flesh and spirit. That was the moment of life. What was conquering the dense resistance of material things, or coming off victor in bouts with men? The moment of life is when the infinite sea opens before the lover.

The heart of the island held them like the heart of Allah. The pines sang around them.

"We must go on," spoke Lily. "It is so dark we can't see the Indian on the trail."

"There isn't any Indian on the trail now," laughed Maurice. "You can never frighten me with him again."

THE END

www.ingramcontent.com/pod-product-compliance
Lightning Source LLC
Chambersburg PA
CBHW030808020726
47499CB00006B/1817